SECRET of Squaw Rock

The Shadow Creek Ranch Series

1. *Escape to Shadow Creek Ranch*
2. *Mystery in the Attic*
3. *Secret of Squaw Rock*

SECRET
of Squaw Rock

Charles Mills

REVIEW AND HERALD® PUBLISHING ASSOCIATION
HAGERSTOWN, MD 21740

This book was

Edited by Raymond H. Woolsey

Designed by Bill Kirstein

Cover Illustration: Joe Van Severen

Type set: 11/12 Century

PRINTED IN U.S.A.

97 96 95 94 93 92 10 9 8 7 6 5 4 3 2 1

R & H Cataloging Service
Mills, Charles Henning, 1950–
Secret of squaw rock.

I. Title.

813.54

ISBN 0-8280-0700-4

Dedication

To Luella Kuebler,
one of my most
enthusiastic readers!

This one's for you, Grandma.
With love.

Contents

CHAPTER ONE

INVITATION

✦✦✦

"Come on, Darick," the police captain urged with a touch of frustration in his voice. "I can't force you to go. But it's either that or juvenile detention. And I know how much you like detention. Last time you were there you fell two stories from a window ledge and broke your leg. You're lucky it wasn't your neck."

The 16-year-old Black boy shrugged. "It was raining," he said, a wry smile creasing his thin face. "If it hadn't been raining, I would have made it."

"Made it where?" Captain Abernathy pressed. "Back on the streets? Back to your buddies in the gang?"

The officer looked away from the boy sitting beside his battered old desk and sighed. "Darick, I'm just trying to help, that's all."

"Why?" the teenager questioned, leaning forward. "Why do you want to help me? We're not friends. I don't even like you."

The captain smiled. "You don't have to like me. I just think you're better than the streets."

"So you're trying to be the old man I never had?" Darick laughed. "Forget it. I don't need no father watching over me. I can take care of myself."

"Oh, you're doing a wonderful job of that," the captain nodded, picking up a sheet of paper. "Let's see. Your record shows two arrests for breaking and entry. Two for vagrancy. One for driving a motor vehicle without a license. And one for purse snatching . . ." The man paused and looked up at the teenager. ". . . on the Staten Island Ferry? Darick, where did you think you were going to run to? It says here an old man with an umbrella pinned you down and held you until the boat docked and the police came and took you away. That was plain stupid."

Darick lifted his hands. "It looked like an easy grab. I guess I forgot where I was. And believe me, that old codger was strong. He must have been in the Marines or something."

Captain Abernathy tossed the paper down on the desk. "Do you want to be a criminal all your life?" he asked. "Do you like having police officers chase you up and down the streets of Manhattan? Is that fun? My men don't especially like it. They've got better things to do."

Darick shook his head. "Hey, you don't know what it's like. You get to eat three meals a day. When I get hungry, I can't just trot over to the old refrig and stand there trying to choose between frozen pizza and cheese soup. I gotta hunt for my food, or find the bucks to buy it. What do you know about that kinda life?"

"I know plenty," the officer said flatly. "You think you're the only one who's been hungry in this city? I grew up on the streets. My dad left me and my mom when I was 9 years old. But I didn't go around stealing from hardworking people so I could eat. I earned my way. I worked. I went to school every day and studied my lessons, and took care of my mother until she died in my arms."

Captain Abernathy pointed his finger at the teenager. "So don't feel too sorry for yourself. You're not alone in this world. There are a lot of people hungrier than you."

Darick studied the man thoughtfully. "OK. I'll give you that you understand what it's like. We might have stuff in common. But I don't want to grow up and be a cop. This ain't my idea of making it in the world."

The man looked around the cluttered room. "You don't make it in an office building, or a fancy high-rise apartment. You make it here, in your head. You create your own success. Only you can judge whether your life is on the right track. So let me ask you, Darick, how's your life? Are you on the right track?"

With a shrug Darick stood and walked to the window. He watched the flow of cars, buses, and trucks beyond the panes of glass, and listened to their muffled roar. "I ain't got that many choices," he said quietly. "The streets sorta take them all away."

"As I see it, you have one left," Captain Abernathy said, lifting an envelope and holding it at arms length. "Don't be a fool, Darick. Take it. Make life happen for you. You might not get a chance like this again."

The boy turned and stared at the envelope. "What if I fail there, too?" he asked hesitatingly.

"Then at least you tried. We'll both know that."

Darick slowly reached out and took the envelope.

"You leave tomorrow morning," Captain Abernathy said. "I'll have one of my men pick you up at 8:00."

The boy walked to the door and paused. Looking back at the captain he spoke, his words not much above a whisper. "Do you really think someone like me can change?" he asked.

Captain Abernathy nodded. "That's up to you. Personally, I think you can do anything you set your mind to."

Darick smiled weakly, turned, and disappeared through the doorway.

* * * * *

"Well, what do you think?" Fifteen-year-old Janet Omara glanced over at her twin sister, Joyce. "We have to decide today, you know."

Joyce fingered her soft, dishwater-blonde hair. "Hey, it's up to you. I'll go if you go."

"I'm not going by myself, that's for sure," Janet retorted.

The two girls sat on one of the grassy knolls sprinkled about Central Park, their bicycles resting in the shade of a nearby oak tree.

Occasionally, a jogger would puff by, interrupting the warm summer day with the staccato sound of rubber against asphalt. Then the runner would disappear around a bend, leaving only the distant rumble of traffic filtering through the breezes.

Janet nodded slowly, just enough to cause her ponytail to bob back and forth. "It might be fun. I mean, we've never been any further away from home than Newark."

Joyce pursed her lips and sucked in her breath. "Yeah, but it could be a drag. Besides"—the girl lifted her chin and batted her blue eyes—"we're just two innocent young ladies from New York City." Raising her fingers to her lips and blowing softly, as if to dry nail polish, she added, "It may not be best suited for our refined and proper selves."

A teenage boy approached the girl's bikes. "Hey," Janet shouted in his direction. "Touch those and we'll break your elbows."

The boy backed away, palms raised, then continued down the path.

"I mean," Joyce urged, "we have to consider if the environment would be appropriate for our more, how shall I say, our more sensitive, delicate natures."

Janet belched loudly. "Yeah. We can't be too careful about such things."

The girls looked at each other and burst out laughing. Falling back against the grass, they rolled in its sweet-smelling softness.

After the giggles had eased, they lay side by side, each lost in thought. The envelopes had arrived just a week ago. Even now they were tucked away in a corner of their bedroom, in the wall, behind a loose board.

Ever since they were children, all their secrets had been hidden there; ticket stubs from their one night at the Ice Capades, a ball-point pen once used by a schoolmate whose father had met Ronald Reagan in person and even shook his hand, a few mushy valentines stolen from the most popular girl in school, a wrinkled picture of a guy they'd both fallen for at the same time, a 1921 dime they'd found on the sidewalk, and a small bottle of seawater sent by a friend in California.

Now, two white envelopes, sporting a distant return address, lay beside the other treasures, waiting for their attention.

"What about dad?" Joyce asked.

"What about him?" came the quick reply.

"What if he says we can't go?"

Janet lay still for a long moment and watched a sea gull flap overhead, his form dark and lonely against the overcast sky. Turning to face her sister, she spoke without emotion. "I hate him."

Joyce nodded. "He'll probably say no."

The girl with the ponytail sat up and stretched her legs. "I'm hungry," she announced, abruptly changing the subject. "How 'bout an ice-cream cone?"

"We don't have any money."

"When's that ever stopped us before?"

Thirty minutes later the two girls were riding their bikes slowly along East 79th Street on their way to Lexington Avenue. In their right hand each held an ice-cream cone, the rich, sweet taste of which offered welcome relief, both from the hunger in their stomachs and the warm, moist air that rose from the sidewalks.

"That old man never learns," Joyce called between licks. "I don't know how he stays in business."

Janet nodded and peddled around a taxicab, ignoring the blare of its horn. "He didn't have chocolate. I wish he'd had chocolate."

The two sisters continued up the street, enjoying the ill-gotten and very drippy treats.

Arriving at their apartment building on East 96th, they carried their bikes up the stoop and entered the old dwelling. With much huffing and puffing, they climbed the stairs to the third floor. From the end of the dark hallway they could hear the percussive beat of a radio blaring out a heavy metal song.

"Hey, Mrs. Parkenson," Janet called, trying to be heard above the din. "You've got your radio turned up too loud."

"What?" An elderly woman's head poked around a doorway.

"You've got your radio turned up too loud," the girl repeated.

"Can't hear you," the woman called back. "I think I've got my radio turned up too loud."

Janet waved and smiled. With a shrug, the woman closed her door.

The twins continued up to the fifth floor, bicycles tucked under their arms. By the time they arrived at their apartment door they were both totally out of breath.

"We've got to spend more time at the spa," Joyce breathed.

Janet giggled and pushed open the door. "Hey, Dad, we're home," she called out as they rolled their bikes to a spot between the threadbare couch and the wall. "Have the maid start supper. I feel like having fettuccine Alfredo tonight. Extra garlic."

"Again?" the other twin sang out. "We had that last night, or was it Monday, after the ballet?"

A loud bang jolted the two girls into silence as a man burst from the bathroom. His face was unshaven, dirty, sweating. A stained and torn undershirt draped over his sagging shoulders and chest.

"Where have you two worthless, good-for-nothings been?" he said, punctuating his words with obscenities. "Don't you know what today is?"

Janet turned and faced the man looming above her. "No, Father, what day is this?"

The man's face grew almost purple in rage. "It's wash day. WASH DAY! You're suppose to do the laundry. Remember? I don't have any clean clothes to wear. No shirts. No pants. No nothing."

The girl held her ground. "Were you planning on going out somewhere?" she asked quietly. "Like maybe to look for a job?"

Joyce's breath caught in her throat as she saw the man's hand rise above his head and slam down hard across her sister's face. Janet fell backward against the sofa but quickly returned to her feet.

"Because if that's where you were going to go," she continued, spitting blood along with her words, "I'd have washed every piece of filthy underwear you own." Janet stared at her father, her eyes cold, expressionless. The man returned her gaze, his face frozen in a hateful grimace.

"You worthless dog," he snarled. "How dare you talk to me like that!"

The girl lifted her hand to her mouth and touched the deep cut in her lip. "How should I talk to you?" she asked quietly.

"I'm your father," the man shouted. "You should respect me."

Janet turned and walked toward the hall. Pausing by the kitchen she spun around and faced the man. "You want respect?" she asked. "Then stay away from me. You hear me, Daddy dear? You stay away from me and Joyce. Don't you ever touch us again. *Not ever!*"

With that, the girl continued down the hall, Joyce at her heels.

Once in their room, Janet fell to her knees beside her bed. Ripping the floorboard away from the wall, she grabbed the envelopes and held them out to her sister.

"We're going," she announced firmly. "And nothing will stop us."

* * * * *

A heavy rain was falling on Chicago's South Side as a young boy walked along the main shopping street of Englewood. With hands thrust deep into the empty pockets of his worn jeans and raindrops saturating his faded Cubs sweatshirt, the 13-year-old lad should have felt miserable.

But not Ruben Manuel Alfonso Hernandez. Miserable was the last way he wanted to feel.

A smile spread across his sun tanned face. Straight white teeth grinned in playful mockery of the pouring rain. So what if he didn't have a cent to his name? So what if he'd just been told that his afternoon bagging job at the grocery store was being terminated because of "employee cutbacks"? So what if his friends thought he was crazy? He was going away, to a place he'd never been before, to a place where there were mountains. He'd never seen one.

The closest he'd ever come to being on anything that remotely resembled a mountain was when he'd taken his grandmother to the top of the Sears Tower. He used two week's earnings from his summer job to ride up the elevator and treat them both to supper in a restaurant with glass plates and menus without pictures on them.

It was an evening he'd never forget. Grandmother still talked about it. The view from the observation room had been breathtaking. The two had pressed their faces against the glass and stared down on the city sprawled at their feet.

Ruben had traced Lake Shore Drive as it ran beside Lake Michigan, past the Museum of Science and Industry, past Washington Park, Soldier Field, the harbor piers, and north to Wilson Beach.

Turning west, the old woman and the boy had gazed at the setting sun as it fell behind the distant ruler-edged horizon. Car lights had sparkled in the streets far below as the city's army of business men and women headed home for the evening, leaving their tall office buildings empty in the soft glow of street lights and the moon.

"It is so beautiful," Grandmother had said in Spanish, the only language she knew. "I almost feel like God looking down at the people of the world. From here it doesn't seem so bad."

Ruben had nodded. "Yes, Grandma. Maybe God has better eyes than we have. I hope so. From here you can't see our house."

The two had stood by the thick glass until the night sky filled with stars and their stomachs reminded them that supper was in order.

Reluctantly, they'd returned to the speedy elevators and soon were seated in one of the smartly decorated restaurants at the base of the towering structure.

Ruben smiled at the memory.

Suddenly he felt a hand on his shoulder. "Hey, Hernandez. What's your hurry?"

The boy found himself surrounded by eight wet teenage faces.

"I'm just headin' home," he said, trying to continue his journey.

"No, you're not," another voice called out. "We've got a job tonight. Should be a good one."

Ruben ignored the invitation. "Not interested. Got plans."

"Yeah?" a large boy grabbed him by the shoulders and spun him around. "Like what? What plans do you have that don't include us?"

"Come on, guys," the boy urged, growing a little irritated, "I'm not going with you tonight. I've got to get home to my grandmother. She's waiting."

"Oh," voices called mockingly. "Gotta take care of old granny. What a baby."

Ruben looked about the group. "Just go," he warned. "Leave me alone."

One of the bigger teenagers in the group approached the boy.

"What's gotten into you, Hernandez? You goin' soft on us? Hey, fellas. Hernandez is goin' soft." The boy reached out and pushed at Ruben's chest. "Can't take it anymore, is that it? You scared? 'Fraid the cops will catch you?" Turning to the others, the big teenager said with a whine, "Hernandez is afraid."

Laughter erupted from the gang. Ruben glanced about the group, his eyes steady, unflinching. Without saying a word, he turned to continue his walk.

"Hey!" voices cried out. "We're not finished with you yet, you little wetback."

Hands gripped him by the arms and neck and suddenly he found himself being dragged into an alley between two buildings. He was half thrown against a brick wall; the impact sent a shot of pain down his leg.

He spun around and faced the members of the gang. With the flick of his wrist the oldest boy brought a knife blade up in front of Ruben and held it there, waving it slowly back and forth.

"So you don't want to play with us anymore," the bully teased. "Well, you just can't leave this gang. No, no. You have to fight your way out. It's the rule."

Ruben glanced around at the others. Their expressions reflected the scorn imprinted across their leader's frowning face.

The cornered boy knew the rule all too well. South Side gangs swore by it. If you wanted out, you had to fight your way to freedom.

Ruben slowly reached into his back pocket and pulled out a smooth, shiny object. He pressed a small button at one end of it and instantly a blade flipped out and clicked into position.

The two boys began moving slowly, around and around, their eyes staring at each other in deadly concentration. The rest of the gang formed a circle about the combatants and stood silent, unmoving, waiting to see what would happen.

A car skidded to a stop at the far end of the alley and two police officers jumped out. Seeing the new arrivals, the gang members turned and fled, almost falling over each other in their haste. The leader, his hand grasping his knife, took a swipe at Ruben, sending him crashing into a collection of trash cans with a long, thin cut across his chest.

Then the attacker turned and ran after the others, leaving Ruben under a pile of garbage.

One of the policemen sauntered over to the messy mound of refuse and sat down on a cracked, wooden box. Rain dripped from his visor as he studied the pair of legs protruding from the heap.

"Hello, Ruben," he said.

After a long pause a voice responded from under the discarded papers and rotting rubbish. "Hello, Captain Perry."

The policeman shook his head. "Having a party, were we?"

"No, sir," came the quiet answer. "I was just headin' home."

"I see," the officer said. "Friends of yours?"

"Sorta."

Captain Perry knelt beside the pair of legs and began lifting some of the garbage off the fallen teenager. "You know, Ruben, I'm surprised at you. Thought you knew better than to pick a fight with eight guys all at the same time."

"I just never learn," the boy sighed.

Gently removing the last layer of rubbish from Ruben's face, the officer was greeted with a sheepish grin.

"You're a mess," the man stated flatly. "Your grandmother's not goin' to like that you dirtied up your sweatshirt—a Cubs one at that. And look. Somehow you managed to get it and yourself cut. I'm not so worried about you, but the shirt—it's a real shame. I like the Cubs."

Ruben chuckled. "Since when?"

The police officer helped the fallen boy to his feet. "Since they knocked the pants off the Phillies last season. My ex-wife lives in Philadelphia. I hate Philadelphia."

Captain Perry examined the gash across the boy's chest. "Ever since then, they've been my heroes."

Ruben nodded and waved to the other policeman waiting by the squad car. "Cubs are great," he enthused. "Been following them ever since I was a kid."

"That long?" Captain Perry lifted a limp leaf of lettuce from the boy's shoulder. "Ever seen 'em play?"

"On television. Once I saw their chartered bus drive by, but it was night and I couldn't see inside. I waved anyway."

The policeman motioned for Ruben to follow. Together they stepped over the toppled metal cans and headed for the car. "I saw them play at Wrigley once," Captain Perry announced. "Astros. Cubs beat 'em 8 to 4."

"Imagine that," Ruben laughed.

"Houston's a good team! They just need some help in the outfield, and . . . on the mound, and . . . in the dugout . . ."

When the two reached the car, Captain Perry took

a small plastic first-aid kit from the back seat and flipped it open. His partner held a large umbrella above their heads, shielding them from the pouring rain. "Now let's see if we can fix you up so your grandmother won't have a heart attack when she sees you."

With gentle hands the policeman cleaned the wound with disinfectant from a spray bottle and then placed a wide strip of white gauze across the cut. Next he stretched lengths of adhesive tape along the bandage and pressed it firmly against the boy's skin.

Stepping back, he eyed his work critically. "You'll live," he announced. "It wasn't too deep. Just a scratch."

Ruben looked down at the bandage. "Thanks," he said. Glancing up at the officer he added, "I didn't start the fight. Really."

"I know," the man said. "We've been watching you."

"You have?" Ruben gasped. "Why?"

"Wanted to make sure you stayed alive until tomorrow. You still have the envelope, don't you?"

"Yes, sir!" Ruben smiled broadly. "My airplane leaves in the morning."

The police officers nodded and slipped back into their car.

"Oh," Captain Perry called out as the engine roared to life. "I almost forgot. This is for you." He tossed a plastic bag from the window and waved as the vehicle eased out into traffic and disappeared around the corner.

Ruben returned the wave, then opened the unexpected gift. There, tucked in the corner of the bag, was a brand new sweatshirt with a Cubs insignia printed boldly across the front. A note read, "To a happy tomorrow."

The boy leaped into the air with a mighty war whoop and sped down the sidewalk, his face glowing with joy. He'd toss his old faded and torn sweatshirt in the dumpster by his house. Now, with this new gift, he'd be leaving in style.

* * * * *

A bright southern California sun shone down on the carefully clipped lawns and flower-decorated fences along Coldwater Canyon Drive as it wound its way through Beverly Hills. To the southeast, the modern spires of Hollywood, Wilshire, and Los Angeles rested below a thin layer of smog that snuggled between the San Gabriel Mountains and the Pacific Ocean.

On each side of the winding road stood aristocratic mansions. Their vine-covered faces, proud and timeless, peered from behind tightly locked gates at a long, white limousine that floated by. From the back seat of the gleaming automobile, 13-year-old Andrew Albert Morrison III stared through the darkly tinted window. His finely-featured face presented a storm of frowns.

"Stop that," his mother said when she glanced over at him. "Makes you look a like a war orphan." The woman took another sip of the bubbly liquid in her cut glass, high-stemmed goblet and continued reading the newspaper.

Andrew rolled his brown eyes and let his head bump against the headrest. "I don't want to go," he said firmly.

"What's that, dear?" the woman asked, looking up.

"I said I don't want to go."

"Of course you do," she sighed.

"Mother, it will be awful. I just know it. I will probably hurt myself. I bruise easily, you know."

"You won't hurt yourself," the woman argued. "And even if you do, they'll certainly have doctors somewhere around. Doctors are everywhere."

The boy stomped his foot on the carpeted floor. "Why do I have to go?"

"Andrew, we've already been over this," Mrs. Morrison moaned. "How many times do I have to tell you? You either accept the police chief's invitation or your name gets put in the paper. It was very nice of Mr. Mott to give you this choice."

Andrew folded his arms across his monogrammed shirt. "Why would they put my name in the paper? I didn't do anything wrong."

The woman shook her head. "I don't know what the big fuss is, either. It wasn't a very large hole."

"I guess I used too much powder. I told William it was too much powder."

Mrs. Morrison gazed out the window. "Maybe it was the man across the street—you know, that Mr. Cho. I don't think he was any too pleased that the explosion shattered the front of his store. Your father and I offered to pay for all damages, but no-o-o-o. He and that jewelry store owner got nasty. They were totally unreasonable." She sighed. "Rodeo Drive proprietors tend to be that way."

The woman smiled over at her son. "Tell me again why you and William decided to blow a hole in the wall of that store. You could have just walked in during the day and purchased anything you wanted. Your bank account isn't exactly lacking, you know."

Andrew nodded. "It was going to be a surprise for your birthday. There was this lovely pin. It had a horse carved on it, along with gold leaves and a fence.

Outstanding workmanship."

"Oh," the woman gasped. "Sounds exquisite. I really appreciate the thought behind your action. Next time, just use your Visa card."

The limousine pulled up in front of a sprawling mansion. Stained glass windows and a wide wooden porch adorned the entrance. Flowing marble stairs led to tall arching doors.

"But why this?" Andrew whined as he stepped from the car and held up a white envelope. The police chief had handed it to him the day after his midnight "shopping spree" at the jewelry store. "Isn't this cruel and unusual punishment? I mean, what if I get lost, or something big bites me?"

"You'll be just fine," the woman encouraged. "You can call me on your cellular phone every day. If I'm not in, my service will know how to contact me."

She turned and looked lovingly at her son. "We mustn't forget the Morrison name. It wouldn't look good in the paper, now would it? Your father would be the laughing stock of the club. I couldn't face my friends anymore. It would be just awful!"

"I suppose," Andrew agreed halfheartedly, walking into the broad lobby of his home. "Who knows, this might be fun, in a simple, redneck sort of way. I understand they have horses."

"There, you see," the woman brightened. "You'll fit right in. You rode a horse once. Even trotted a few paces. I was so proud."

Andrew reddened. "Oh, Mother. You embarrass me."

"That's what mothers are for," she said, her lips pursed in a mock kiss. "Now go find Sarah and tell her to pack your things. We have to have you at the airport early tomorrow morning. Your father has reserved the company jet." Glancing at the envelope in her son's hand she added, "I hope the pilot knows where to find this . . . this . . . Where are you going?"

Andrew glanced at the return address. "Montana," he said.

"Yes, that place," the woman nodded. "Now, run along. And don't forget your blue blazer. It's so . . . so . . . cowboy. You'll look stunning, wearing it on the back of a horse."

CHAPTER TWO

Zoo

✦✦✦

A wooden box sat at one end of a field. Bread crumbs lay on the ground around it. One side of the box was propped up by a small, forked aspen branch. The other end of the branch had been pressed into the soft bottomland soil.

A large rope, its coarse fibers coiled in a knot around the center section of the branch, snaked away from the box, through the green summer grass, over a small boulder, around a cottonwood tree, and disappeared over the lip of the shallow bank that led down to a sun-sparkled creek.

Mud-stained fingers held the rope tightly as a dark-skinned face peered from behind a bush. A blue jay squaked from a nearby spruce, causing the prone form on the creek bank to stir.

"Sh-h-h-h," the little girl hissed, frowning up at the noisy intruder. "Go away. Just go away."

The blue jay ignored the pleas and hopped from

branch to branch for a closer look. He tilted his handsome head from side to side as if to say, "What on earth are you doing?"

The girl gazed intently at the distant box. Nothing yet. But something would come along any minute, she was sure of that. What animal in his right mind could resist bread crumbs?

To sweeten the deal, the hunter had even spread a little peach jam on some of the larger pieces of bread. Now that would make any bait irresistible!

A movement in the bushes not far from the box caught the girl's attention. Even the blue jay noticed the disturbance. He left abruptly, sending a chorus of squawks and screeches over his shoulder. Strong wings carried him to the branches of a tall willow at the base of a hill beyond the creek.

The hunter pressed herself closer to the ground until just the top of her head showed above the bank. What was coming to her trap? A fox? A mountain lion? Maybe even a bear! The girl's body tensed. She listened for sounds.

Yes, she could hear something eating. Slurp, slurp, slurp. Her fingers tightened on the rope. Crunch, crunch, crunch. She waited, holding her breath in excitement.

Slowly she raised her head until the distant box came into view. A movement under the wooden slats confirmed her expectations. Some creature had entered her trap!

With a mighty yank, the little girl pulled the rope as hard as she could.

The branch holding up one end of the box snapped away and the crate fell with a muffled thump to the ground.

"I did it. I did it!" the girl squealed as she raced up

the bank, past the cottonwood, around the small boulder, over the grass, and to the spot where the box lay on the ground.

Something definitely was inside. She could hear a series of snarls and gurgles as a furry form bumped against the side of the enclosure.

The little girl moved slowly toward her trap, her head tilted to one side. "Hello," she called. "I'm not going to hurt you."

The animal in the box stopped its thrashing and became motionless.

"See, it's just me. I'm your friend. Did you like the bread crumbs? I've got more. Peach jam, too."

A pair of dark eyes peered from between the wooden slats.

"Would you like some more bread crumbs?" The girl knelt beside the box. "I can't see what you are. Maybe you're a groundhog or a fox. I think you're too little for a bear, unless you're a little bear, and that would be OK."

The diminutive hunter reached out her hand to lift the box slightly so she could get a better look at her prize.

"I'm just going to take a peek at you. Don't worry. I won't—"

Some sort of liquid spray emerged from the box and splattered against the little girl's face and chest. Suddenly, her eyes began to burn and she coughed.

Drawing in a deep breath she almost fell over backward. A strong, horrible odor, an odor her 4-year-old nose had never smelled before, an odor so awful, so pungent, that it seemed to lift her from the ground and drop her again, this indescribable odor pressed around her with such vengeance that all she could do was sit there, unable to move.

The animal in the box peered from between the slats. He lifted his own nose and sniffed as if to say, "I did spray, didn't I?"

All at once the girl let out a scream. She jumped up and began running across the pasture.

Inside the box the animal sighed with relief. "Yes, I guess I did," it seemed to say.

A big white house stood at the far end of the valley. The long driveway leading to its green lawn and broad front porch skirted a grove of fruit trees and ran along the creek.

Joey Dugan sat on the veranda eating an apple, enjoying the warmth of the summer sun. He glanced up when he heard the far-off shriek.

"What was that?" he asked his friend and ranch boss, Barry Gordon.

Barry looked up from his book. "What was what?"

Another scream echoed across the valley.

"That!" Joey said, jumping to his feet. "Sounds like Samantha."

The two raced down the steps and along the driveway. They could now see the little girl stumbling through the fruit orchard, bumping into low-lying limbs and trunks.

"Hey, something's wrong with Samantha!" Joey called, his voice urgent.

Closing to within 100 feet of the girl, the two boys suddenly stopped in their tracks. "Whew! What's that smell?" the younger boy coughed, his face twisted into a grimace.

"Skunk," the wrangler announced, lifting his fingers to hold his nose.

Samantha saw her brother and Barry by the driveway. "Help me," she called.

The two boys began to back away slowly. Then they

turned and ran toward the Station, the name given the old inn by the creek. "Hey," Samantha gasped. "Don't go away. You gotta help me!"

Two girls appeared on the porch. They'd been drawn from their chores by the commotion outside.

"Look at that," blonde-haired Wendy called to her older sister, Debbie. "Samantha is chasing Joey and Barry up the driveway. Must be some new game. They sure are making a—" The girl coughed. "What's that awful smell?"

Debbie backed away from the steps. "Yuck. Smells like . . . like . . . I don't even know what it smells like!"

The younger of the two gagged and sputtered, waving her hand in front of her face. "How can a little girl have such a big smell?"

"I don't know," Debbie choked, "and I'm not sticking around to find out."

The two ran back into the Station and slammed the door behind them.

"What's going on?" Lizzy Pierce called from the direction of the big kitchen. "Do I hear Samantha screaming?" The old woman emerged from the dining room, her hands encrusted with bread dough.

She stopped in her tracks. "What's that terrible stench?"

Grandma and Grandpa Hanson clambered down one of the two curving staircases in the high-ceilinged lobby. "Has everyone gone mad in the front yard?"

The couple hurried to the wide door and opened it just as Joey and wrangler Barry burst through. When he got a whiff of the odor that followed the boys in, Grandpa Hanson slammed the door shut again.

Samantha, who had reached the front yard, saw the door slam. She stopped and stood at the base of the stairs. Faces appeared at the sitting room window.

Lifting her tear-stained chin, she cried up at the big Station, "Help me. I STINK!"

"Boy, that's for sure," Wendy coughed. "She smells like . . . like . . . all the bad smells I've ever known rolled into one."

"She must have had a run-in with a skunk," Grandpa Hanson announced, his voice filled with pity.

Joey held a handkerchief over his nose. "Poor baby. She looks so little there at the bottom of the steps."

Grandma Hanson scratched her head thoughtfully. "We can't let her into the Station or we'll all smell like that."

Samantha saw someone lean over the second-floor porch. "Well, hello, Samantha," Mr. Hanson called. "What are y—"

The man backed away as if struck by some unseen hand. He waved weakly, coughed, and returned to his office without another word.

"Hey!" Samantha shouted, her fists planted firmly on her hips. "What's going on? Isn't anybody going to rescue me?"

The front door opened a crack. "Samantha, dear," Grandma Hanson called from behind a dish rag. "Could you move away from the house a little? We're going to help you, but you must be patient. Go down and stand by the creek."

Wendy's face appeared below her grandmother's. "No, Samantha. Go down and stand *in* the creek."

The door quickly closed.

Samantha's bottom lip quivered as she turned and walked slowly toward the footbridge that arched across the sparkling waters separating the broad front yard of the Station from the horse pasture.

As she approached the creek, the dozen horses loitering near the gate lifted their heads and snorted.

In one accord they turned on their hooves and galloped across the pasture to the stand of cottonwoods at the base of the mountain. From there they looked back at the little girl waiting knee-deep in the cool waters of Shadow Creek.

In the Station, Joey was slipping out of his shirt and pants and shoes and socks and was pulling on one of Grandpa's old bathing suits. Debbie laughed out loud when she saw him emerge from his bedroom and waddle up the hall past the dining area.

"You look like a turtle with skinny legs," she teased.

Joey ignored her taunt. With a weak wave he drew in a deep breath, opened the front door, and slipped out onto the porch. The door clicked shut behind him.

"Sam?" he called as he headed down the steps. "Yo, Samantha. I'm coming to rescue you. See? Here I come."

The girl looked up and saw her brother waddling across the lawn. She lifted her hand to her mouth and giggled. "Why you wearing those big pants?" she called out.

"Well," Joey encouraged, "we've got to get your clothes off and then we'll bury them, with these pants, in the ground. Then the smell will go away. That's what Grandpa Hanson says."

"We're going to bury my clothes?"

"Yup." Joey gingerly walked down the bank and stumbled to his sister's side. "You stink awful," he said, holding the handkerchief over his nose.

"The animal in the box peed on me," Samantha announced with a shake of her head.

"Nah," Joey encouraged. "He didn't pee on you. That was a skunk, and he just sprayed you with some stuff he uses to chase away animals who are trying to eat him."

"I wasn't going to eat him," Samantha giggled.

"He didn't know that," Joey said with a shrug. "Come on, now. Let's get these clothes off you real fast."

The little girl lifted her arms as Joey gingerly pulled her stench-ridden shirt over her head. With a plop her shorts fell into the swift-flowing stream, leaving her standing in her underwear.

Gathering the garments, Joey led his sister up the bank and across the footbridge. They hurried over to the horse corral and found a shovel. Moments later, the offending clothes were deep in the ground.

Then the two moved back to the Station and paused by the porch where a hose and bucket of soapy water waited. They had been hurriedly placed there by Grandpa Hanson after Joey had left the house.

Bubbles of lather rose from the soft brown skin of the little girl as Joey scrubbed and scrubbed her arms, legs, and narrow shoulders. Then he turned the spray of water on himself, cleaning his hands and arms as best he could.

After the vigorous bath was over, Samantha still carried a rather strong reminder of her encounter with the skunk. Joey did too, but to a lesser degree.

When dinnertime rolled around, they were invited to dine alone beside the creek. With these precautions, the Station and its occupants had been spared the fragrance freely offered by the little creature in the meadow.

After the excitement had calmed, Wrangler Barry hurried out to free the captured animal and return it to the wild. This was accomplished with a very, very, long stick. The little black and white captive ambled off into the bushes, grateful to be out from under the wooden box.

Joey bit down on his sandwich and eyed his sister. "Why were you trying to catch a skunk? That ain't such a good idea."

Samantha spooned soup into her mouth. "I didn't know I'd catch a skunk. I wanted a mountain lion or a bear."

Joey constrained a chuckle. "Well, why do you want to catch anything? You have Pueblo the puppy, you know."

"Some friend he is," Samantha pouted. "When he saw me running in the pasture, he turned and headed into the forest. Haven't seem him since."

Joey laughed. "He'll come back. Maybe he didn't like your particular brand of perfume."

"I guess," the little girl nodded. "But I was trying to catch animals for my zoo."

"You gotta zoo?" the boy asked.

"Yeah. In the tack house."

"Well, how many animals you got in it?"

Samantha thought for a minute. "None. That's why I was trying to catch a mountain lion or a bear."

"Tell you what," Joey announced, finishing off the last remnants of his meal. "I'll help you find some other animals to put in your zoo. Like, maybe a butterfly or grasshopper. Would that be OK?"

"You'll help me?" the girl asked, brightening.

"Sure. They won't let us in the Station until tonight. We can spend the afternoon hunting. Just me and you. OK?"

"OK," Samantha squealed, jumping to her feet. "Maybe we can catch a buffalo!"

"Let's just stick to the smaller creatures of the forest."

With that the boy and little girl headed across the footbridge. They paused long enough at the corral to get a net and some cans. Then the two hunters strode out into the wilds of Shadow Creek Ranch, ready to do battle with any and all creatures waiting among the summer leaves and wind-swept grasses.

* * * * *

Bozeman buzzed with its usual blur of afternoon activity as Tyler Hanson and his father steered the minivan into the Hotel Baxter parking lot.

Slipping from the seat, Mr. Hanson stood and watched the flow of cars and trucks. He shook his head. "You can know I've been away from Manhattan for a long time, when this looks like a traffic jam."

His father smiled and leaned back into the van to retrieve a brown briefcase. "New Yorkers would consider our Main Street a regular fast lane."

The two men walked down the sidewalk and entered the seven-story structure. With a wave to the receptionist they crossed the lobby and continued up a flight of stairs to the second floor. They entered the office of Ms. Ruth Cadena, director of Project Youth Revival, a privately-funded program that Shadow Creek Ranch had joined forces with during the winter.

The petite, dark-haired woman behind the desk smiled when she saw the two men at her door.

"Tyler, Mr. Hanson, come in," she invited with a broad smile, motioning toward a couple of chairs by the wall.

The visitors made themselves comfortable as their host rose and closed the door behind them.

"Today's the day," she announced happily.

The younger Hanson shook his head. "I can't say I'm not a little nervous. But this is why we came out here from New York. This is why Shadow Creek Ranch was created."

The woman nodded. "You'll do just fine. I've seen your ranch, I've talked to all your people. I can't think of a better place for these youngsters to spend their summer."

Grandpa Hanson flipped open his briefcase. "Here's the final curriculum we've planned," he said, handing a small pile of papers to the woman. "Your suggestions worked in with no problem at all."

Ms. Cadena glanced over the documents. "You folks are certainly organized."

"We're lawyers, Ms. Cadena," Mr. Hanson smiled. "Comes with the territory."

"Now, I've told you to call me Ruth," the woman scolded cheerfully. "Ms. Cadena makes me sound like an old widow woman. Please. Just Ruth."

Mr. Hanson nodded with a touch of shyness. "OK, . . . Ruth."

"Good," the woman responded, a faint blush reddening her olive-skin cheeks. "Now, back to business. Your guests will be arriving at the airport in about an hour. They all caught connecting flights in Salt Lake City, except the one from Los Angeles. He's arriving by private jet."

Grandpa blinked. "Must be nice."

Ruth laughed. "His dad's a real estate developer in L.A. Money is not a problem in their house."

Pushing aside a pile of papers, the woman continued. "You should have an interesting summer. All your kids are very special in their own way. That's why they were selected.

"As I told you when we began the process, we work very closely with the police departments in the major cities supporting our program. Only those children who show a true potential are selected. The policemen involved feel the boys and girls can benefit from their visit to a place such as Shadow Creek Ranch."

The woman paused. "These kids need a break. They need to get away from their environment for a while, to gain a new perspective on life. Some are abused. Some have had run-ins with the law. But they all need a chance to grow, to learn how to better handle the life they're forced to live. The ranch is not a prison, it's a school, a place where these boys and girls can learn a little more about themselves.

"They're not dangerous. Oh, they may have done stupid things, but they're just searching for something to believe in. That's what Project Youth Revival tries to provide, with the help of kind people like you."

Grandpa Hanson nodded slowly. "We'll do our very best."

"And, hopefully, the kids will realize that," Ruth added. "I'll be coming out once a week to check on things, to talk with the kids and you folk. We'll work together all during the summer."

Mr. Hanson leaned forward in his chair. "What are we looking for? How will we know if we're succeeding in reaching our young guests with anything worthwhile?"

"You'll know," Ruth said with a gentle smile. "You'll know it in your heart. And so will the boys and girls who come to you for help."

* * * * *

Debbie tilted her head to one side and studied the room thoughtfully. She wanted everything to be just right for the new arrivals when they reached Shadow Creek Ranch.

Grandma Hanson poked her head in the door.

"Looks great," she encouraged. "I like the flowers. Adds a very sophisticated touch."

The girl with the long dark hair nodded. "Ms. Cadena said the twins would appreciate having flowers in their room. They've always lived with their dad in a small apartment near Central Park. She said the two like to walk around the lake after school. Maybe this will remind them of home. I hope so."

Grandma Hanson smiled and looked about the freshly painted room with its wide, lace-curtained window overlooking Shadow Creek and the horse corral. "You've fixed the place up just right. They'll love it. How 'bout the rooms on the boys' wing? They ready to go?"

Debbie motioned for her grandmother to follow. Together they walked down the hall, crossed the upstairs balcony overlooking the foyer, and entered the north wing of the Station.

Several more rooms on the second floor of the old stagecoach inn had been renovated, along with bathroom facilities.

"What do you think?" Debbie asked, opening a door. "This one's for the boy from New York. I put a picture of Manhattan on the wall. Don't want him to get too homesick."

"Now if you could just play a recording of a taxi honking its horn we'd be all set," Grandma Hanson quipped as she surveyed the carefully panelled walls, rustic desk, and comfortable bed.

A refinished antique dresser, rescued from the Station attic, leaned against the wall by the window. Glancing past the tan-colored curtains she could see the ground rise to the road running above the Station and then continue up the hill to the mountain tops beyond.

"Very nice," the woman said nodding.

The two made their way to the next room. "This one's for the guy from Chicago," Debbie announced. "I put a book about Illinois on his desk. I had a hard time finding a picture for his wall. The closest I could come was a photograph I took while we were driving by his city on our way out last fall. Daddy had it enlarged. It just shows a long line of trucks out on the freeway."

Grandma Hanson bent and studied the photograph hanging above the dresser. "It'll make him feel right at home, I'm sure."

Finally the third room was inspected. "This is for Mr. Hollywood," Debbie giggled, sweeping her hand out in front of her in a royal gesture. "I've got movie stars, Disneyland, and a poster from 'The Sound of Music.' "

The older woman whistled. "Terrific! The little desk lamp shaped like a movie light is a nice touch. And I like the curtains. Palm trees. Yup, this is great. You've done a beautiful job on all the bedrooms. I'm right proud of you, granddaughter."

Debbie blushed. "I hope our guests like them, too," she said.

Wendy joined the pair and glanced into the chamber. "This is all wrong," she moaned. "We need this particular room to look like an earthquake's just hit. We can call it Suite 205, The Big One."

"That theme has already been taken," Debbie retorted. "Check out where you and Samantha dig yourselves in at night. Now, that's mass destruction."

Wendy shrugged. "It's just our very specialized way of being organized. Samantha and I know where everything is. Works for us. In your room, even the dust particles have assigned places."

Debbie opened her mouth to respond but closed it

again. She smiled down at her sister, turned, and walked toward the balcony overlooking the foyer.

"Grief," Wendy sighed. "I hate it when she acts like a big sister."

Grandma Hanson laughed. "She is your big sister. She's 17. You're 10. Remember? Had a birthday party and everything. Samantha gave you a dragonfly."

Wendy grinned. "How could I forget. It got out of its jar and flew out the window. Samantha started to cry and I told her the poor bug was just answering the call of the wild. She bought it."

Grandma chuckled. "Where is Samantha, anyway? I wonder if she's still . . . uh . . . how shall I say, intensely odoriferous."

"I don't know about that," Wendy shrugged, "but I hope she doesn't still stink to high heaven. She and Joey headed for the hills after lunch, right before Dad and Grandpa went into Bozeman. They're probably out trying to find another Sarabell."

"Sarabell?"

"The dragonfly that answered the call of the wild."

"Oh, yes."

The two laughed and headed for the foyer. It was almost time for Shadow Creek Ranch's first official guests to arrive.

Tar Boy and Early stood by the cottonwood grove, munching on soft summer grasses. Their tails switched from side to side, sending the swarms of flies, trying to hitch a free ride on their gently sloping backs, buzzing into the air.

Around them, ten other horses grazed contentedly, their soft chewing sounds reflecting the enjoyment they were feeling over their meadow meal.

Suddenly, Early's head jerked up, followed by Tar Boy's and then the others. A distant cloud of dust heralded the approach of a vehicle from behind the Station.

The animals watched as a little red minivan traveled the bumpy path cut into the hillside above the inn's north wing. The automobile followed the road that descended slowly down the length of the valley. It turned onto the long driveway, passed by the fruit orchard, and headed back toward the Station.

Soon, with a grind and a jolt, the vehicle came to rest in front of the sturdy structure.

Grandma Hanson and Lizzy appeared on the porch, followed by Debbie and Wendy. They stood at the railing, expectantly surveying the collection of new faces that emerged from the minivan.

Ms. Cadena looked up at them and waved. "Come on down and meet your guests," she invited with a happy grin.

The women descended the stairs and approached the van. Five young people stood in a tight group, their faces showing a mixture of uncertainty and total amazement at the beauty surrounding them.

"Welcome," Grandma Hanson said, extending her hand. "We're so glad you've come to spend your summer with us."

Debbie and Wendy waved shyly. The group waved back.

Ms. Cadena pointed at the new arrivals and motioned for everyone to gather around. "Let me introduce these young people to you. First, this is Darick Tanner, from New York, and these are the Omara sisters, Janet and Joyce, also from New York City. Yes, they're twins.

"Over here is Ruben Hernandez, from Chicago, and this is Andrew Morrison, from Beverly Hills, California."

Ms. Cadena continued her introductions. "I'd like you to meet Debbie and Wendy Hanson, Grandma Hanson, and . . . and . . . where are the others?"

"They're out catching bears," Wendy said quietly.

"Bears!" Ruben gasped. "You have bears here?"

"Oh, sure," Wendy nodded. "Mountain lions, too."

Debbie stepped forward. "Don't listen to her," she urged. "She has a wild imagination. But we did see a bear print out in the meadow this spring. It was this big." The girl held her hands about 12 inches apart.

"Wow!" gasped Joyce. "Did you ever see the actual animal?"

"Nah," Debbie smiled, shaking her head. "Montana bears are more afraid of us than we are of them. Same for mountain lions."

There was visible relief in the faces of the new arrivals.

"It's beautiful here," Janet breathed. "I love the mountains."

"Yeah," Ruben added. "We don't have too many mountains in Chicago. Just Lake Michigan. It's kinda neat."

The group was silent for a minute. Mr. Hanson and the other adults stood to one side, watching and listening.

Andrew approached the girls. "I was talking with your father on the way in from the airport. He says he has a home office here. I have a computer with a modem and everything."

"Well," Debbie said lifting her hands, "I don't know anything about that sort of stuff. Dad's the expert."

"Yeah," Wendy interjected, "my sister only knows about dresses and fashions. Stupid stuff like that."

"Oh," Andrew said, looking down at his feet.

"You like fashion?" Janet asked. "I like it, too.

Well, I don't have any neat stuff to wear, but I like looking at pictures. Joyce and I want to be fashion designers, or maybe even models."

"Me, too!" Debbie cried. "But you don't have to buy your clothes. You can make them. Come on, I'll show you my sewing machine. Got it for my birthday last February."

The three girls hurried up the steps, talking excitedly.

Wendy watched them go. "Brother. What sissies. I personally prefer baseball."

"You like the Cubs?" Ruben said shyly, pointing to his new sweatshirt with the team's colorful insignia painted across the front. "They're my favorite. Chicago, you know."

"They're OK," Wendy shrugged. "I prefer the American League."

Mr. Hanson stepped forward. "Hey, speaking of baseball, how 'bout a game of catch before supper? We've got some gloves and balls in the Station. Wanna play?"

Ruben and Wendy brightened. "Sure," they chorused. "Hey, Darick, Andrew, you can play, too."

Andrew shook his head. "I'm no good at sports. Besides, I bruise easily."

"I'll bet you do," Darick said coldly.

"Hey, that's OK," Mr. Hanson encouraged, smiling over at Andrew. "Why don't you go up to my office and check out the equipment? You can fax your mom and tell her you arrived safely. I'll come up and join you later."

Andrew grabbed his leather suitcase and overnight bag. "Thanks. I love computers." Then he paused. "By the way, where is your office?"

"I'll show him," Grandma Hanson offered, then

turned to the boy. "And I'll take you to your room, too, so you can settle in a bit."

The youngster eagerly followed the old woman up the steps and disappeared into the Station.

"How 'bout it Darick?" Mr. Hanson urged. "Join us for a game of catch?"

"Nah," the teenager said with a wave of his hand. "I'll just go over here and look at the horses."

With that he turned and shuffled in the direction of the pasture.

"Where's Joey?" the lawyer whispered under his breath. Lizzy lifted her hands. "He and Samantha are off hunting for wild game. Been gone all afternoon."

"Well, I wish he'd come back. He could show Darick around." The lawyer paused. "Wait. I think I see them out by the cottonwoods." The man cupped his hands over his mouth. "Hey, Joey."

A distant figure glanced up and waved. Lizzy saw him reach down and take his sister's hand. Together they began walking up the valley, toward the Station.

"Good," Mr. Hanson smiled. "Everyone's accounted for. Let's play ball."

He, Wendy, and Ruben headed for the Station to collect some gloves and a ball while Ms. Cadena and Grandpa Hanson set about unloading the van.

Lizzy walked toward the footbridge. Even from a distance she could tell the couple in the pasture had a heavy load of cans and small boxes. Hunting must have been fruitful.

"Look, Dizzy," Samantha called out as the brother and sister approached the corral. The old woman smiled. Samantha and Joey always called her "Dizzy." It was a name the boy had bestowed upon her years before when they were living in the same apartment building in East Village, a run-down neighborhood hiding in the shadows of Manhattan's tall towers. Joey's 2-year-old tongue hadn't been able to manage a proper "L" sound so her name had become Dizzy.

"Look, Dizzy," Samantha called again, a broad smile lighting her dark face. "See? We caught lots of critters for my zoo. We got butterflies, grasshoppers, two green-and-brown lizards, a bird feather, and a bug that we're not sure what it is. Oh, and we got a mouse. Joey almost stepped on it."

Lizzy peered into each can and box, uttering appropriate "ohs" and "ahs" with each glance. "That's quite a collection you've got there," she enthused. "You'd better get them something to eat. They look hungry."

"OK," the little girl nodded, carefully balancing a load of creatures in her muddy arms. "Barry said I could have my zoo over in the tack house. He made me a shelf and everything."

Joey and Lizzy watched as the diminutive hunter charted an erratic course toward the small shed beside the corral. The old woman bent and sniffed Joey. "I can still smell that awful skunk, but not as much as before. I think it's safe for you and Samantha to come into the Station again. Sorry we had to keep you out all afternoon."

"That's OK," the boy chuckled. "I don't blame you. We did stink pretty bad. I guess the sunshine and breezes have helped clear the air a little."

"Well, hurry back to the Station. Our guests have arrived."

"Oh, great!" Joey said, picking up the remaining can-cages. "We'll be right there."

Lizzy nodded and returned to the Station as Joey and his sister busied themselves setting up the little zoo under the tack house window. Soon all the creatures were bedded down on clean, soft grass. Tiny containers of fresh water waited nearby, ready to quench any thirst the zoo inhabitants might develop.

Samantha glowed with pride as each miniature member of her menagerie settled into his or her new domain.

"We'd better hurry," Joey urged. "I want to meet the new kids at the Station. Come on, Sam. Let's go."

The little girl waved a happy good-bye to the rows of jars and cans, then skipped out into the sunlight.

Joey ran ahead, lifting his arm to his nose, testing to see if all the odor had dissipated. There was still a lingering scent, but at least it wouldn't gag anyone.

As the boy hurried across the footbridge he heard someone call his name.

"Hello, Dugan. Long time no see."

The color drained from Joey's face as he spun around. A tall, slender boy was standing down on the bank beside the creek, a large stick held firmly in his hand.

"Darick Tanner," Joey gasped, his eyes not leaving the new arrival.

"Small world," Darick called back.

Joey stood rooted to the spot as Samantha ambled up beside him. "Who's that?" she asked.

The boy on the bridge positioned his sister behind him. "Go back to the corral Samantha," he said quietly, evenly.

"Why?" the little girl asked. "I want to—"

"Samantha," Joey said firmly. "Just go back. Do what I say."

The girl shrugged and headed toward the pasture gate.

Darick moved slowly up the bank and stood at the base of the footbridge. In one swift movement Joey slipped his hand behind his back. It emerged with his hunting knife held tightly between his fingers.

Darick didn't flinch. "Just like the good old days," he said. "You, me. 'Cept I don't got no knife. You wouldn't cut a guy who's got no knife, would you?"

Joey licked his lips. "I've seen what you can do with your fists," he said, trying to fight the dizzying fear pressing against his head. "You didn't become a gang leader because of your good looks."

Darick lifted the heavy stick and tapped one end of it against his open palm. "No, I guess I didn't. It might have been my outgoing personality. Can I help it if everyone likes me?"

Joey glanced back at his sister. She was just entering the tack house. "Or maybe it was because you cut up everyone who tried to stand against you."

The boy moved backward along the footbridge as Darick edged toward him.

"Well, now it's just you and me, Dugan. No gangs, no turf, no nothing. Just you and me."

Joey's eyes narrowed. "If you want to fight me, Tanner, I'll fight. But what good would it do? I mean, we're not in New York anymore. You have nothing to prove here."

Darick shrugged and continued his slow approach. "Oh, I imagine we could think of some reason or another. Maybe just for old times sake. I heard you'd gone soft. Sure didn't know you'd come clean out here to this dump."

"Shadow Creek Ranch ain't no dump. And I didn't go soft. I just found something better than the streets."

"Oh?" Darick sneered. "Maybe that dark-haired chick . . . what's her name . . . Debbie? Is that why you left New York?"

"You leave her out of this. She's my friend."

Darick faked a forward lunge. Joey stumbled back,

his knife shining in the afternoon sun.

"Come on, Dugan," the boy urged, "you can level with me. What scam you workin' out here in the middle of nowhere?"

"There ain't no scam," Joey responded, anger building in his chest. "This is pure legit stuff, something you wouldn't know anything about."

"So you really think you can help guys like me see the light? Very big of you."

Joey felt the hard wooden slats of the pasture fence press into his shoulder. He stopped and glanced past Darick toward the Station. Lizzy appeared on the porch and looked in his direction. The boy saw her hand fly to her mouth as she spun around and hurried back through the front door.

"So come on, Dugan," the aggressor said dryly. "Let's have at it right here, right now. Or are you scared? I never knew Joey Dugan to be scared."

Grandpa Hanson and his son burst from the Station door and sped down the steps.

"I don't want to fight you," Joey said quietly. "It doesn't do nobody no good."

"Just like I thought," Darick responded with a sneer. "You've turned chicken."

The boy lifted the stick and lunged forward. Joey sidestepped as the wooden weapon slammed against the gate, sending splinters flying.

"Come on, Dugan," the boy urged. "Let's see what you've got. I wanna know how much of the old Joey is still in you. You used to be pretty good with a knife."

"That was before," Joey said angrily. "I ain't like that no more."

Mr. Hanson shouted across the footbridge. "Darick, Joey, stop right now!"

Darick lunged again, his stick whistling just above

his intended victim's head.

"Stop it!" Mr. Hanson shouted. "I mean it!"

Joey backed along the fence. "You heard him," he urged. "This is stupid."

The boy with the stick continued his attack. "Since when is a fight stupid? I saw you that night in the Village. Remember Paul? Well, he remembers you, every time he looks into the mirror and sees where you cut his cheek open like a side of beef."

"That was a long time ago," Joey shouted. "I don't do that no more."

Darick swung again. "Once a fighter always a fighter," he said.

The stick glanced Joey's head, just above the ear. The boy fell back, his vision blurring.

Suddenly, a form descended on his attacker. Mr. Hanson grabbed Darick and spun him around. The boy lifted his big stick to strike.

"Do it and you're in jail!" the man warned.

Darick stood, arms raised, weighing the words just spoken. Slowly he lowered the weapon and let it drop to the ground. Mr. Hanson bent and picked it up. Glancing at Joey, he tossed it into Shadow Creek.

Grandpa Hanson joined his son. "Now, what was going on here?" he asked sternly.

Darick shrugged. "Just a little friendly game."

"Oh, sure," Joey said, stumbling to his feet. "You don't play friendly games. You've always been dead serious."

"Put the knife away," Mr. Hanson ordered.

"Hey, Mr. H, you don't know this guy."

"Put it away, Joey."

"But you can't trust him!"

"PUT THE KNIFE AWAY. NOW!" The man glared at the boy.

Joey blinked, his mouth open in shock. Mr. Hanson's angry command had surprised and embarrassed him. Never had his friend spoken in such a cold manner.

He searched the lawyer's face, but found no hint of compassion. The man waited, his jaw set firmly.

Joey began to lower the knife, then paused. Looking straight at the lawyer he called out, "Anything you say, hotshot."

With a flick of his wrist, Joey sent the knife slicing through the air. A sharp twang rang out as the blade imbedded itself deep into the wooden gatepost inches from the lawyer's arm.

Wordlessly, the boy turned and walked past Darick and the others. Somewhere in his chest a long-forgotten anger flared to life and began to burn once again.

CHAPTER THREE

SQUAW ROCK

✦✦✦

Supper dishes clanged and rattled as Debbie and Wendy worked through their list of evening chores. The new arrivals had been instructed to make themselves at home in the Station, to unpack their bags, and to explore the pasture and creek. Tomorrow, they'd be assigned chores, too. But for now they could relax and get to know their surroundings.

Ms. Cadena occupied her time getting to know the guests, visiting with them in the warm evening shadows.

Joey had remained quiet during the meal. As soon as his duties were done he slipped away to the corral and began saddling Tar Boy.

Wrangler Barry arrived from town just as the teenager was placing the bridle over his big black horse's nose.

"Hi, Joey," the wrangler called as he entered the corral, arms laden with supplies.

Joey nodded without turning.

Barry paused, then lowered his head. "I heard what happened this afternoon. Glad no one was hurt."

The boy shrugged.

"I guess lawyer Hanson came down pretty hard on you. Sorry."

Joey turned and faced his friend. "That's his problem."

"Whoa now, wait a minute," the wrangler cautioned. "Don't judge the man too harshly. He's not used to breaking up fights, I mean, real fights. Somebody could have been injured bad."

"I can take care of myself," the boy said, adjusting a stirrup.

The wrangler watched his companion work. "Joey," he said softly, "no one's perfect. Even folk we care about make mistakes. Maybe Mr. Hanson overreacted a bit. Can't you forgive him? I hate to see you two at odds with each other."

"Look, Barry," Joey said as he led Tar Boy out of the corral. "I thought Mr. H trusted me. I thought he believed that I was good inside. But this afternoon he showed me his true feelings. I could see it in his face. As far as he's concerned, I'm no better than Darick Tanner. So why try to be?"

The boy hoisted himself into the saddle. "I don't need no Manhattan big-time lawyer playing judge over me. Either he trusts me or he doesn't. It's as simple as that."

Tar Boy lunged forward as Joey dug his heels into the animal's sides. The two thundered out of the pasture and swept across the footbridge. With a resounding slap of the reins the rider and his steed raced past the Station and galloped up the long driveway, pounding hooves echoing along the mountain side and across the meadow. In moments they were gone, leaving behind a thin cloud of dust hanging in the air.

A man stood on the second floor balcony of the Station. His face reflected the anguish in his heart. He'd let the boy down. He knew that. In his desperation to stop the fight before anyone had gotten hurt, he'd forgotten to remember Joey's feelings, his sensitive nature, the very qualities that had drawn him to the lad many months before.

Mr. Hanson lowered his eyes. *Why*, he thought, *why did I treat him so coldly? Why did I shout at him like that? Joey wasn't going to use the knife. He was just trying to protect himself. I didn't trust him. I let him down. I let my friend Joey down.*

"Hurts, doesn't it?" A soft female voice called from the direction of the office.

Mr. Hanson turned to find Ms. Cadena standing in the doorway.

He smiled weakly. "You heard what happened, huh?"

"Yes. But don't be too hard on yourself," the woman encouraged. "It was a bad situation."

Mr. Hanson threw up his hands. "I'm no good at this. The first day and I blow it. Darick thinks I'm some sort of parental bully and Joey . . ." the man's voice cracked. "Who knows what damage I've done to him."

Ms. Cadena walked across the porch and stood beside the man. "Let me tell you something, Tyler," she said quietly. "If a person exists who can always do the right thing at the right time, I don't know about him. We're human. We make mistakes. We say things, do things that we shouldn't. We blow it, big time. And people, people we love, suffer. That's just the way it is."

The lawyer gazed out across the valley. After a long

pause he spoke. "Will he forgive me?"

"Joey? Oh, he might need a little prodding. But I'm not so worried about him. It's you that concerns me."

Mr. Hanson turned to face the speaker. "Me?"

"That's right," the woman said. "The most important question you have to answer is, can you forgive yourself?"

The man looked down and studied the handrail thoughtfully. Running his fingers across the smooth, polished wood he said, "I don't know. I'm not too good at that, either."

Ms. Cadena placed her hand on his. "Loving troubled children is not so much about our feelings for them. It's how we accept ourselves that counts. You're a good man, Tyler Hanson. Don't forget that.

"This afternoon, Darick and Joey gave you a glimpse into their world. It frightened you. Now they need for you to show them your world. Let them know that violence and anger doesn't have to exist. There are alternatives. You must try to do this because, if the truth be known, there by the footbridge they were the most frightened of all."

Mr. Hanson nodded slowly, then smiled. "How'd you get to be so wise?" he asked.

Ms. Cadena chuckled. "Life has taught me many things. But the most important lesson this ol' heart of mine had to learn is to ease up on myself. You might want to do the same. It can save you lots of pain."

The woman turned and walked across the porch. At the door she paused. "Make life happen, Tyler. Don't wait for things to straighten themselves out. They never do."

Mr. Hanson smiled. "Thank you, Ruth. You're a good friend."

The woman shrugged. "That'll do for now."

With a wave she continued through the office and out into the hallway. The lawyer turned and gazed toward the distant peaks, now bathed in bright moonlight. The stars were out. A warm feeling stirred in the man's chest. Did Montana stars always shine so brightly?

Joey reined in his horse and slowed to a trot. The night air felt fresh on his face and arms. In the moonlight he could see the road clearly, each rock and blade of grass sharply outlined by its own dark shadow.

The boy rode on, letting his hurt feelings simmer in the beauty of the evening.

In all the world, there was only one man who had shown him any degree of concern. Mr. Hanson had been different, special. A guy would have to search a long time to find such a friend.

But all that love had seemed to vanish into the Montana air. Joey sighed angrily. What had happened? Why had the lawyer turned on him so? The event had embarrassed him deeply. He thought he and the lawyer were better friends than that.

Rounding a bend, the boy looked up and saw the stone formation this particular canyon had been named for. High on the skyline, dark and mysterious in the silver light of the moon, was Squaw Rock, a towering image made of granite and shale.

He and the others had been here before. They'd always admired the graceful lines and rugged contours of this structure carved by centuries of rain and wind.

From the road, the rock looked just like an old Indian squaw sitting on a huge boulder. She leaned forward slightly, a crooked cane in her hand. A few pine trees grew from her shoulders and lap, like bristles on a porcupine. At her feet a pile of loose rock lay scattered, as if the old woman had been cracking nuts and letting the shells drop to the ground.

Behind the formation the mountain continued to rise, creating a broad, living background to the curious image.

Joey slowed his horse to a walk and sat looking up at the rock as they approached it. Red Stone, the ancient Indian who lived on Freedom Mountain not far away, insisted that the old woman guarded a sacred burial ground, hidden somewhere in the surrounding forest.

Over a crackling fire, the man had spun stories like a spider's web, encircling his listeners with wonder and amazement, and a twinge of fear from time to time.

Joey recalled the old storyteller's face as it turned and tilted in the firelight.

"Many mysteries in the mountains," the Indian had said, his faltering English adding to the impact of his words. "At night, when moon is full and stars shine and shadows climb the cliffs, you can hear whispers at The Squaw. What voices are saying, no one knows. It strange language."

The old Indian had paused and looked around his dark cave. "But beware the eyes. On these nights, they shine. The Squaw restless when eyes shine in the moonlight."

Joey shivered a little. The ancient storyteller could make your skin crawl with his raspy voice and tales of spirits whose mournful whispers rode the wind.

Suddenly, Tar Boy stopped, almost tossing his rider forward over his broad neck.

"What's the matter?" Joey asked, patting the horse lovingly.

The animal seemed to grow nervous, his hooves stumbling across the road.

"Hey, Tar Boy, what's the matter?" Joey asked again.

The big horse began to back up slowly as if something in the path was frightening him.

Joey slapped him firmly on the rump. "Come on, animal," he said. "What are you backing up for?"

Tar Boy rose on his hind legs and pawed the air with his hooves. It was then that Joey glanced up at the formation looming ahead. His breath caught in his throat. The eyes of the squaw were glowing as red as fire, as though in a wicked sneer. The whole formation seemed to be leaning forward, as if to reach out and grab the rider and his steed.

The boy screamed, his voice echoing across the valley and up the distant mountain sides. With trembling hands he yanked hard on the reins and spun his horse around. Without looking back he raced down the road, his body pressed flat against the surging neck of the animal.

Behind, the eyes of the squaw dimmed. And then, as if giant lids were lowered, the light was gone, leaving the rock formation bathed only in moonlight and encircled by the stars.

Daybreak found all but one of the Station inhabitants deep in slumber, each enjoying the softness of their beds and the cool breezes flowing through their open windows.

Wendy sat in her favorite porch chair, feet up on the railing, sipping a glass of orange juice and patiently waiting for the sun's first appearance. She always got up before anyone else. Her dad often suggested that she was the original morning person. Debbie insisted she was just a bat.

The girl sighed contentedly as she caught sight of Early out in the pasture, grazing on the dew-covered grasses. He moved in and out of the fog that had formed above the waters of Shadow Creek and now floated aimlessly along the valley floor.

Another dark form by the cottonwoods caught her eye. The girl gasped as she recognized Joey's windbreaker and baseball cap.

Rising, she skipped down the steps and hurried across the footbridge. What was he doing up so early?

"Hey, Joey," she called when she was halfway across the dimly lit pasture. "What are you doing? I thought you hated mornings."

Joey glanced up and waved weakly. "Hi, Wendy," the girl heard him say.

Drawing nearer, she noticed his face was smudged, his shirt dirty. Come to think of it, he hadn't been in the Station at all last night. Everyone figured he was sleeping out in the corral.

"Where you been?" she asked.

"No where," came the quiet reply.

"You still mad at my dad?"

Joey rolled his eyes. "Does the whole world know what happened between him and me?"

Wendy thought for a minute. "Well, parts of East Africa haven't checked in yet, but, yes, I'd say that everywhere else, the problem's being discussed."

"Very funny," the boy said. "But your dad is only one of my worries."

"Oh? So, what made you stay up all night? You look like a Montana mountain fell on you."

Joey glanced around and stepped closer to Wendy. "I . . . I saw something. Something awful."

"Ah," Wendy said waving her hand, "that was just

Debbie. A little lip gloss, a little blush, and she perks right up."

"No," Joey whispered, moving even closer. "I saw something up in the mountains."

"What?" the girl blinked, suddenly very interested. Wendy liked a good mystery. "What did you see?"

"Promise you won't say anything to Samantha or the others?"

Wendy raised her right hand. "I promise."

"Well," the boy continued, "last night, late, I was up by Squaw Rock. I was remembering what Red Stone had said about the place and . . . and . . ."

"And what?" Wendy urged.

"I saw it. It happened just like he said it would. The moon was full, the stars were shining, there were shadows on the cliffs, and I looked, and the old woman's eyes were shining, blood red. Tar Boy saw it, too. Spooked him bad. He almost threw me off his back. We turned around and got out of there as fast as we could. Scared the aspen sap out of me. Never seen anything like it before in my life. That rock formation had eyes and they were open!"

Wendy drew in her breath. "Wow!" she whispered. "Red Stone was right. You must have been near the sacred burial grounds."

"Then you believe me?" Joey said hopefully. "I mean you really believe me?"

Wendy nodded. "Of course. I figured out the curse this spring, didn't I?"

"Well, it wasn't really a curse," Joey countered. "We just thought it was."

"Yeah, yeah, yeah. But this. This is real. You saw the old woman's eyes glowing just like Red Stone said they would. Man, this is neat. This is really neat!"

Joey let out a long sigh. "Then I'm not crazy!"

"Well, I wouldn't say that, but you saw what you saw." The girl paused. "And I'm going to see it, too." She grabbed Joey's arm and pulled him close to her. "Listen, the moon will still be full tonight, and the weather is supposed to stay clear for at least three more days. You're going to show me exactly where you saw this . . . this . . . thing happen. We'll go together, you and me, tonight, OK?"

Joey rubbed his chin. "I don't know. It was pretty scary."

"Hey," the girl urged, "stop worrying. You'll have me there. Besides, you want someone else to see it, don't you? Then you'll know for sure that it wasn't a dream or something."

"It weren't no dream, that's for certain," the boy said, shaking his head.

"Good," Wendy smiled. "We'll saddle up and leave at the same time you left last night. Should get to the Squaw around the same time, too. Oh, this is great. Red Stone strikes again!"

Joey shrugged. "I guess it's OK. I mean, the curse turned out to be nothing but so much Indian folk lore. I'm sure there's a logical explanation for what I saw, too."

The boy stiffened. "But, what if there are real ghosts up there? What if Red Stone is right and they come after us?"

"Then we'll outrun them with Tar Boy and Early. Not even a dead person can catch us when we're poundin' down the valley."

Joey nodded slowly. "OK. Meet me in the corral at 8:00. And don't let anyone know what's going on."

"Thanks, partner," the girl said, thrusting out her hand.

The boy shyly accepted her handshake. "And don't call me partner," he said.

"OK, compadre."

"That either."

The two walked through the mist toward the distant Station.

"How 'bout comrade?"

"Just call me Joey. My name's Joey."

The fog swallowed them up, leaving the pasture glowing in the first light of day.

"How 'bout chum? buddy? pal? associate?"

"Joey! Just Joey!"

* * * * *

Darick Tanner opened his eyes and sat up. He blinked. Where am I? he mused. Tilting his head to one side, he gazed at the picture of the Manhattan skyline hanging on the wall above the dresser. Where'd that picture come from?

Then his thoughts began to gel. *Oh yes. I'm in Montana. Montana! Sounds like a foreign country.*

He listened. No traffic sounds drifted in through his bedroom window, just some tweeting noises. Birds, he figured.

The boy swung his feet over the side of the bed and sat rubbing his eyes. Wait. Shadow Creek Ranch. Now he remembered. This joint is suppose to help me change from bad boy to Boy Scout.

Darick chuckled to himself. Oh, well, I promised ol' Captain Abernathy I'd give it a try.

Stumbling sleepily to the window, he gazed out at the hillside. *I'm really off to a good start*, he encouraged himself sarcastically. *I've already managed to get Dugan and that lawyer mad at each other. Everybody thinks I'm a real jerk.*

He shook his head slowly from side to side. *But the last time I saw Joey Dugan, he was fighting a bunch of hoods in an ally off East 27th. Didn't do too bad, either. How was I suppose to know he got religion?*

Darick sighed. *They're gonna send me back to New York for sure.*

A gentle knock rattled his bedroom door. "Hold on," the boy called as he quickly slipped into his faded jeans. "I ain't decent." Brushing the wrinkles from his shirt, he walked to the door and opened it. Mr. Hanson stood in the hallway, a glass of orange juice in his outstretched hand.

"Here," he said, "thought you'd like some juice to wake you up."

Darick eyed the offering. "Uh . . . yeah . . . sure . . . thanks."

The boy took the glass and smiled nervously. Mr. Hanson motioned toward the room. "May I come in? I'd like to talk to you."

Darick shrugged. "Your house," he said.

The lawyer followed the tall, slender lad into the room and closed the door behind them.

"Listen," the man began, "we . . . uh . . . kinda got off to a bad start yesterday, you know, down by the footbridge. But, I can't have you fighting with Joey, or anyone else for that matter."

The speaker sighed. "Our goal is to make sure everyone has a good time here at Shadow Creek Ranch. We're all new at this. You guys are our first guests."

Mr. Hanson paused, then continued. "Darick, I'm used to arguing corporate cases, not stopping knife fights. So, could you give me your word you won't start anything with Joey or the others? I realize you're probably used to being the leader of a gang, but we don't have a gang here. We have a group of kids who need to have a fun summer.

"You're the oldest guest. If you want to be a leader, that's fine. Just remember who your followers are. Life's been hard on them, too."

Darick stood looking at the lawyer. Had he heard right? They weren't planning on sending him back to the city?

"Sure," the boy stammered. "I'll take it easy. Just tell Dugan to stay out of my way."

Mr. Hanson waved his hands. "No. You see, that won't work. He can't stay out of your way because this is his home, too. You guys have to learn to live together under one roof without trying to draw blood every time you bump into each other. I mean, you don't have to be bosom buddies or anything. Just try to tolerate one another, OK?"

Darick nodded. "I will if he will."

"Yes, well," the lawyer turned to leave, "I've got to work that out, too. But I'm glad you're willing to help in this situation." At the door he paused. "Now, you'd better drink your juice and get downstairs. Breakfast is almost ready."

Suddenly a loud bell began ringing. Darick jumped. "What's happening? A fire?"

Mr. Hanson smiled weakly. "No," he called out, trying to be heard above the clanging. "We've got regular fire alarms for that. The bell's Wendy's idea. Suppose to tell everyone that the meal's ready. Overkill, if you ask me."

Darick chuckled. "I'll be down in a minute. Oh," he lifted the glass. "Thanks for the juice."

The lawyer spread his hands apart and smiled. With a wave he turned and walked down the hall.

The breakfast table swarmed with activity. Big

bowls of steaming oatmeal and stacks of sweet-smelling bread waited at the center of the long, wide table. Darick and the twins sat at one end, watching the happy commotion with wide-eyed wonder, just as they had the evening before. Never in their entire lives had they attended meals such as these. There was laughter, good-natured kidding, smiles.

Ruben, the boy from Chicago, had had happy times with his grandmother and other family members in the past. Andrew's mother and father had eaten with him when their schedules permitted. But for the other new arrivals, this breakfast table held an appeal almost as tantalizing as the aroma that filled the room.

Darick looked up as Joey took his place across from him. The two boys glanced around the table, doing their level best to ignore the other's existence.

"Please settle down, everyone," Grandpa Hanson called, lifting his hand. Voices hushed as he bowed his head. "Father in heaven," he prayed, "thank You for this beautiful day. We ask Your blessing on our food. We want to especially thank You for our guests. Help them to enjoy their summer with us. And Lord, clean our hearts of anger and hurt. Make us forgiving and kind. This we pray in Jesus' name, amen."

"Amen," joined in some of the others quietly.

Mr. Hanson glanced over at Joey. The boy looked away and reached for a dish of applesauce. "What are we doing today?" he asked, handing the platter to Debbie.

The girl smiled. "Today we're going to ride horses."

A cheer rose from the assembled youngsters. "Can we run 'em?" Ruben asked breathlessly.

Wendy spooned oatmeal into her bowl. "Not until I say you can," she responded with a maternal air. "I gotta make sure you won't fall off."

Ruben nodded. "OK. But I'm going to ride all day long."

Janet lifted her hand to her forehead. "I can't go riding. I don't have a thing to wear."

Joyce and Debbie giggled. "Today, a fashion statement we are not," the girl with the long dark hair announced. "But there's a cute riding outfit in one of my magazines. We'll see what we can do about our attire when we return from the trail."

Wendy rolled her eyes. "What's wrong with jeans and a sweat shirt? Like the horses care what you're wearing?"

Debbie turned to the twins. "See what I have to put up with?" she moaned. "My little sister is fashion brain dead."

The twins laughed and helped themselves to a tray of biscuits.

Andrew looked over at Mr. Hanson. "Are you going riding, too?" he asked.

"No, partner," the lawyer smiled. "Gotta work."

"May I stay and help you?"

Mr. Hanson blinked. "Don't you want to go riding?" The boy shook his head. "I'd much rather assist you. I noticed you have a new faxboard. I'll be happy to show you how to install it."

"You know how to install a faxboard?" the lawyer gasped.

"Sure. I'll set up the software, too. Piece of cake."

"Well," the man hesitated, "if it's OK with Wendy. She's in charge of the horse lessons."

Andrew turned and faced Wendy expectantly. The girl studied him for a long moment.

"You bruise, right?" she asked.

"Black and blue from head to toe."

"OK with me," she shrugged.

"All right!" the boy enthused. Mr. Hanson smiled and winked in his direction.

Wrangler Barry strode into the dining room, air-drying his freshly scrubbed hands. "Hi, everybody. Sorry I'm late."

Janet and Joyce's mouths dropped open. Debbie leaned toward them. "I told you," she whispered.

The three giggled and nudged each other as the handsome horseman took his place beside Lizzy. Breakfast continued in high spirits. Only the occasional glance between Joey and Mr. Hanson reminded the others that all was not well on the valley ranch. But the promise of blue skies and horseback riding vetoed the tension, as all remnants of the morning feast disappeared down thankful throats.

Joey stood in the corral mending a bridle as Wendy and the others slowly walked their horses around the pasture. He could hear the young girl's voice singing out, giving instructions and encouragement.

The lad smiled to himself. No one could give instructions like Wendy.

"Now, don't get too close together," he heard her say. "You don't want to get your foot crushed. If you do, it'll turn black and fall off."

A moment later he heard, "Good. You're doing very good, except you, Joyce. You're not doing it right. Stop trying to braid your horse's mane. He doesn't like it."

Joey strained as he tried to get the new straps to fit the buckle he was adjusting. Leather wasn't the easiest material to work with.

"Hey, Dugan, I want to talk to you." A familiar voice called from the doorway.

Joey spun around to find Darick's form silhouetted against the bright Montana sun.

The boy froze, his eyes glancing about the room for

some sort of defensive weapon. Anything would do.

"Oh, ease up, man," Darick said. "I ain't here to fight. I just want to talk, OK?"

Joey relaxed a little. "What do you want to talk about?"

The dark-skinned boy strode into the corral, leaving his horse waiting outside. "Look. I don't want us to be at each other's throat all the time."

"Hey, you came at me yesterday," Joey protested.

"Yeah, well, that was yesterday. I didn't understand."

"Understand what?"

Darick sat down on a stool and was silent for a minute. "This place is for real, isn't it?" he said slowly.

"I told you it was."

"I mean, you guys are serious about this ranch for city kids stuff. I ain't never had nobody do nice things for me before. I ain't use to it. Know what I mean?"

Joey laid the leather straps down on the table and shrugged. "So?"

"So, I don't want to mess things up, for me, for the others. I want to make peace with you so we won't jump every time we see each other."

The boy at the table nodded slowly. "Sounds good to me. I'll do it if you'll do it."

Darick smiled weakly. "You're a pretty good fighter," he said. "I seen you back in East Village. You never backed down from anybody. I guess you're OK."

Joey shrugged. "You ain't so bad yourself. I've heard stories about how you and your gang used to go to the warehouses on the river and lift stuff right out from under the noses of the security guards."

The boy on the stool nodded. "Yeah, well, maybe that was dumb. I don't know. We got caught."

The conversation lagged. Darick kicked at a piece

of straw on the floor and looked over at his companion. "You know, you're messin' up a good thing here on the ranch."

"What thing?"

"You and that lawyer guy."

Joey lifted his chin a little. "That ain't none of your business."

"Yeah, I know. But you shouldn't blow a gig like this. I mean, this is a whole lot better than the streets. Here's a guy who likes you enough to step in and stop a fight. How many men do you know in the city who would do that?"

Joey didn't respond.

"The lawyer's an OK guy," Darick continued. "So he gets on your case? So what! I'd be glad if someone took that much interest in me." He slipped off the stool and walked to the door. "Count your blessings, man," he added. "He ain't perfect, but he's a whole lot better than nothing."

Joey watched as his visitor pulled himself clumsily up onto his horse's back. The boy fingered the reins and guided the animal on an erratic course out into the pasture. After a lot of tugging and kicking he managed to head his steed in the same general area as the other riders.

Joey leaned against the wooden door and replayed Darick's words in his mind. "He ain't perfect, but he's a whole lot better than nothing."

With a sigh, the boy returned to his work. Maybe Darick was right, he thought. But how could he make things right with Mr. Hanson? Why was it so easy to get into a fight and so hard to get out of one?

CHAPTER FOUR

GHOSTS

✦✦✦

Mr. Hanson's mouth dropped open and he drew in a sharp breath. Andrew Albert Morrison III looked up from his work.

"Don't worry, sir," he said with a smile. "I can put it all back together again. Really."

The lawyer blinked. "What have you done to my beautiful computer?"

"I'm installing your new faxboard," the boy answered with a shrug. "Remember? I promised I would."

Mr. Hanson sat down heavily in the office chair beside Andrew. "But did you have to take it all apart? Why'd you have to take it apart? Looks like the poor thing exploded!"

"See this?" the lad asked, holding up a circuit board and turning it slowly in his hands. "This is old technology. They have 'em much faster now. *Much* faster. This is like really ancient. You should upgrade."

The man lifted his chin slightly. "But I like that . . .

that . . . thing. It's fast enough for me."

"Well, OK," Andrew said with a weary nod. "But an ST-589, or even a Mark 104 would cut down your seek rate and access speeds and up the old throughput. Have you noticed any fluctuations with your benchmark readings?"

Mr. Hanson stared at the boy for a long moment. "I haven't the faintest idea what you're talking about," he said slowly.

Andrew laughed. "Don't worry, Mr. Hanson. It took me a while to learn this stuff, too. You'll catch on."

The lawyer surveyed the scattered piles of boards, chips, and cables. "When can I have my computer back in one piece? I've got work to do."

The boy's hands began jumping from place to place on the table. "Give me five minutes, and you'll be up and running better than ever."

"Five minutes?" the man gasped. "You can put all that back together in five minutes?"

"Sure, complete with new faxboard. Piece of cake."

Mr. Hanson shook his head from side to side. "You're amazing, Andrew," he said. "How'd you learn to do all this?"

The boy spoke without looking up. "My dad's business partner, Mr. Collins, started to teach me. Then he had to move to Seattle. So I bought a bunch of books and learned some more. I want to be a computer technician after I finish law school."

The man blinked. "Wait a minute. If you want to be a computer technician, why go to law school?"

Andrew inserted a long, chip-lined driver card into a slot on the computer's mainboard and pressed down gently. "My mom says the family needs a lawyer in it." He looked up. "Sort of like you, I suppose. But then I'll start a business building and fixing computers. I'll do lawyer stuff on the side."

Mr. Hanson stifled a grin. "I've been tempted to do that myself. But maybe you'll like being a counselor. Have you ever thought of that?"

The boy continued his work. "All the ones I know are crooks."

Mr. Hanson laughed out loud. "L.A. must be a rough neighborhood. There's good and bad in every occupation. You could be one of the good ones."

Andrew turned a screwdriver slowly between his fingers. "I guess. Do the good ones make more money?"

The man shrugged. "I think they sleep better at night."

The computer screen flickered to life. Mr. Hanson and the lad watched the machine run through its self-test sequence. In seconds, a flashing prompt indicator signaled that all was well within the tightly packed collection of chips, wires, resistors, and jumpers. The artificial mind of Mr. Hanson's computer was awake and ready for input.

"Amazing," the man said softly. "You did it. And my new faxboard is ready, too?"

"Just as soon as you load the software. It's a good board. Fast. You'll like it."

Mr. Hanson beamed. "I'm glad it meets with your approval."

The boy placed the cover on the machine and connected some cables between it and the printer.

As the last connection was made he looked over at Mr. Hanson and smiled weakly. "I really don't want to be a lawyer. Is that OK?"

The man nodded. "You can be anything you choose," he said slowly.

"But what about my mom? I'd rather not make her

upset. She loves me. Thinks I'm wonderful."

"Have you told her your feelings?"

The boy shook his head. "Once. She just said I'll change my mind when I'm older, but I know I won't. I want to build computers. Is that so bad?"

Mr. Hanson leaned back in his big office chair. "This is a tough problem," he said. "Many times parents and kids don't agree on the future. My daughter Debbie wants to be a fashion designer. She's good. I mean, she can make beautiful clothes using simple colors and patterns, stuff I'd never think of.

"But I see the world out there. I know that it's filled with other people who want to do the same thing. Talented people, just like her. I know that if she follows her dream, she might get hurt. Others may walk all over her, say they don't appreciate what she does. She'll more than likely be rejected again and again. That makes my heart ache for her.

"Maybe your mom sees all her lawyer friends raking in the money and she thinks, 'Hey, Andrew should do this.' She doesn't understand computers, so she believes going into that kind of business is too impractical. Your mom wants you to succeed. Lawyers she knows. Computers she doesn't."

"So," Andrew scratched his head, "what do I do?"

"How about if you compromise? You know, meet her half way?"

The boy looked blankly at his companion.

"Let's say," the man continued, "you tell her you want to build computers and write software especially for lawyers. We need good database programs, record keeping programs, stuff we can use to keep our paper work under control. You study into what the law profession needs, and you meet their demands, with software and hardware you design and build yourself."

Andrew's face brightened. "Hey, that's a great idea!"

"It is?" Mr. Hanson gasped.

"Yeah. That way I'm doing lawyer stuff for my mom, and computer stuff for me." The boy thought for a moment. "She just may buy it. I'll write up a proposal."

The lawyer's eyes opened wider. "You're going to write a proposal for your mom?"

"Oh, sure. It's the only way I'll get her attention. She's very busy, you know. I'll keep it short. May I use your laptop?"

Mr. Hanson pointed toward the small, portable computer resting on a nearby shelf. "Be my guest."

The boy settled himself in the chair by the window and switched on the unit. "This is one of those older models," he said happily. "You really should—"

"I know," the man interrupted. "I should upgrade, right?"

Andrew nodded. "I'll see what I can do. They have an accelerator card out that can make this baby really cook. You'll be amazed. Turbo speed and everything!"

The soft hum of computers and spinning hard disks filled the office as the morning sun climbed high in the blue Montana sky. The lawyer and boy labored side by side, each addressing the pressing needs in their lives.

Mr. Hanson scanned a distant database, searching for information regarding a case. Andrew wrote and rewrote words to his mother. Both had a goal. Both were laying plans for the future.

Wrangler Barry ripped open a 50-pound sack of oats and poured the contents into the long feeding trough by the pasture gate. He waited. Sure enough, pounding hoofbeats echoed across the grass-filled expanse between him and the grove of cottonwoods. The ranch's small herd of horses had picked up the scent and were hurrying over for their evening meal.

The young man watched them come, enjoying their fluid movements and eager gallop. He'd spent his entire life around horses. For this native Montanan, pounding hoofbeats mixed with the song of birds was all the music he needed in life.

"Hi, Barry."

A soft female voice called from the footbridge. Debbie approached with Janet and Joyce at her side.

"Evening, ladies," the young man called with a smile. "Is supper ready?"

"Just about," the girl encouraged. "Bean soup and tomato sandwiches. Your favorite."

Barry licked his lips. "Grandma Hanson and Lizzy know their way around a cook stove, that's for sure."

The herd thundered up behind the man and hurried to the oats, almost pushing the wrangler over in their happy haste.

"Hey, watch out, you ugly critters," he called, trying not to be stepped on. "What do you think this is, bean soup and tomato sandwiches?"

The girls laughed as the lean and muscular ranch hand hurried to the gate and passed through it. With a resounding thud, it swung shut, leaving the pasture empty of all human intrusion. Only the crunch of horse teeth against dry oats disturbed the evening calm.

"You'd think they haven't eaten all day," the wrangler mused. "Sorta reminds me of Wendy and Joey at the supper table."

Debbie nodded with a sigh. "They are such children. Sometimes I just don't know what to do with them."

Barry looked up in surprise. "The horses?"

Debbie blinked. "No, Wendy and Joey. They're so

immature. You know what I mean."

"Oh, yeah," the wrangler smiled, a twinkle in his eye. "What we must put up with here on the ranch. I don't know how we survive."

Debbie sighed, then brightened. "Oh, I wanted you to officially meet Janet and Joyce Omara. They're from New York, you know."

"Oh, yes. Very nice to meet you, officially," the young man said, extending his hand.

One of the girls stepped forward. "I'm Janet and this is Joyce. Have you ever been to New York?"

Barry shook his head. "No, never have, although Debbie has told me how nice it is."

"Nice?" Janet retorted. "She said it was nice? It's a dump!"

Debbie cleared her throat. "Well, not all of it. Central Park is OK, don't you think?"

Joyce looked out across the pasture at the distant mountains. "I guess so, but it ain't Shadow Creek Ranch. Now, this is nice."

Barry nodded. "We're right proud of our state."

Janet glanced over at the wrangler. "So, Barry, how long you been a handsome?" Her face reddened. "I mean, a horseman?"

Joyce closed her eyes as Debbie turned her face away from the speaker. Her hand shot to her mouth.

"All my life," the young man said, ignoring the slip. "My father has a spread near Bozeman. They say I could ride before I could walk."

Debbie worked hard to regain her composure. "Barry taught Joey and Wendy how to ride. He even gave me some lessons. I'm not too good at it, though."

"You're a natural," the ranch hand encouraged. "It's just that your heart isn't in it. But that's OK. We each have our own interests. I couldn't design a dress if I tried."

A loud ringing heralded the invitation to supper. Janet turned and whispered over at Debbie. "Saved by the bell!"

The group walked across the footbridge and headed for the big white Station. They'd continue their small talk another day.

* * * * *

The round summer moon rose silent and silvery behind Mt. Blackmore, bathing the cliffs in shadows that moved slowly with the passing minutes.

Not a breath of wind disturbed the late-night stillness. Far in the distance an owl hooted, adding its lonely voice to the timid chirps of crickets and muffled moans of bullfrogs. Stars hung motionless in the sky, their light steady, brilliant in the clean, crisp mountain air.

Joey and Wendy crouched behind a boulder by the road. Early and Tar Boy had been tied to a fallen log some distance back, out of sight of the towering rock formation that loomed above the two visitors.

"See?" Joey breathed. "It's just like before. Full moon. Shadows on the cliffs. Stars. This place gives me the creeps."

Wendy looked around then back at the formation. "Red Stone said we would hear whispers. I don't hear any whispers."

A stray breeze rustled the pine needles above their heads.

"Listen!" Joey gasped. "Maybe that's a whisper."

Wendy cupped her hands over her ears, trying to capture the sound. "Nah. It just says, 'Wheeeeeee.' I don't hear any words or anything."

Joey was silent for a moment. "I don't hear any words either. Maybe the Squaw speaks only Indian. Maybe that's why we don't understand."

"Could be," Wendy nodded. "I'll bet Red Stone would know exactly what the old woman is saying."

A loose rock tumbled from somewhere behind the children and rolled across the road. Joey and Wendy turned and watched it disappear into the bushes.

From beyond the bend, Tar Boy whinnied. Then Early. The two visitors looked at each other. "This is really weird," Wendy breathed.

Joey nodded. "Maybe we'd better head back."

The girl shook her head slowly. "Not until I see the eyes sh—"

Wendy's words caught in her throat as she glanced up at the silvery image a short distance away.

Joey shrugged. "Maybe I was just seeing things. Maybe—"

The girl grabbed her companion and spun him around to face the formation. Joey's cheeks drained of color as he gazed into the brilliantly shining eyes of the Squaw.

"It's real!" Wendy gasped. "It's really real!"

Holding each other tightly, the two fell back from their hiding place behind the rock and stumbled out onto the road. The Squaw seemed to be watching them, her centuries-old eyes glowing red and angry, like fire.

"*Run!*" Joey screamed as he turned and headed down the road toward the waiting horses. Wendy's legs trembled as she tried to keep up. Fear gripped her chest, making her breath come out in short, painful bursts.

As they rounded the bend in the road two white lights emerged from behind the horses and sped toward them.

"She's after us," Wendy screamed, skidding to a stop. "The Squaw is after us!"

The children spun around and raced back up the road, toward the formation. "We're going to die. We're going to die!" Joey repeated over and over as he ran.

The lights from behind came closer and closer, illuminating the cliffs and spruce with a blinding, colorless glow.

"Don't stop," Wendy shrieked, her voice strained and hoarse. "She'll get us if we stop."

Within seconds, the radiant lights were at their heels. In desperation Joey grabbed a heavy stick. With a loud war whoop he spun around, lifted the weapon, and brought it down hard between the two lights.

Clank!

"Hey," a voice called out as the lights weaved to one side and came to a sudden halt in a thick cloud of dust. Joey heard a door open.

"You hit my truck," the voice called out in disbelief. "And this is a new paint job. What'd you do that for?"

Grandpa Hanson stood in the moonlight running his hand over the fresh dent in the hood of his vehicle.

Joey gasped, unable to catch his breath.

"Why'd you hit my truck, Joey?" the old man asked again.

Wendy ran to her grandfather. "Boy, are we glad to see you!" she cried.

"I can tell," the rancher said, glancing at Joey, who stood in the middle of the road, stick still held firmly in his hand.

"Look," Wendy urged. "Look at the Squaw. Look at her!"

Grandpa glanced up at the rock formation. "So?"

"See the eyes?" Wendy challenged, her face buried in the man's arm. "Aren't they terrible?"

"Well, they look like they always have."

Wendy and Joey slowly turned and gazed up toward the image. Squaw Rock sat in the moonlight, her contours etched by the shadows that crept along her shrub-lined shoulders.

The stick slipped from Joey's hand and clattered onto the road. "It's gone," he whispered.

"What's gone?" Grandpa Hanson asked, looking around expectantly.

"The eyes. The eyes have stopped shining."

Wendy looked at her grandfather. "I saw it, too. Really."

"Saw what?"

Joey pointed up the road in the direction of the Squaw. "Her eyes shone just like Red Stone said they would."

"Red Stone? The old Indian?"

"Yeah. He said when the moon is full and shadows creep up the cliffs, the Squaw's eyes will shine to show she's angry that someone is disturbing her sacred burial grounds hidden in the forest. It's true. Wendy and I saw it just a few minutes ago."

Joey moved closer to Grandpa Hanson. "That's why we were running. To get away from the eyes. Then we figured lights from your truck must be ghosts coming after us. So we ran some more. And that's why I hit your hood. I'm sorry. But I was just trying to protect us from the ghosts."

Grandpa Hanson shook his head as if to clear his thoughts. "You thought my truck was a ghost?"

"Two of 'em," Wendy interjected.

The old man sighed. "You guys take the cake. Don't you know there are no ghosts, here or anywhere else?"

Wendy lifted her hand. "But Red Stone—"

"Honey, Red Stone is an old man filled with ancient

Indian folk tales and stories. I'm not saying he's not sincere. He just gets reality a little mixed up with fantasy sometimes."

"But the eyes," Joey insisted. "The eyes shone just like he said. I've seen them do it twice. Last night, and a few minutes ago."

Wendy looked up expectantly as Grandpa Hanson ran his fingers through his silvery hair. "Look, I'll tell you what we'll do. Let's all come up here tomorrow night and we'll see for ourselves."

Joey shook his head. "Can't."

"Why?"

"Won't be a full moon anymore. Red Stone says the eyes shine only when the moon is full."

The old man sighed. "Then we'll come up a month from now, when the moon is full again. OK?"

"You don't believe us, do you, Grandpa?" Wendy glanced down and kicked at a rock.

Grandpa Hanson lifted her chin with his rough, work-worn hand. "I believe you saw something. I do. But it might not be what you think. That's all I'm saying. In a few weeks, we'll come back and uncover the mystery. We'll do it together. Deal?"

"Deal," the children chorused.

Joey turned and faced the darkened formation. "There's a secret up there. I gotta find out what it is." Glancing at his companions he added, "And I hope it's not as painful as the curse was."

Grandpa shivered and held Wendy close to him. "We'll find the answer, but we'll do it together."

Joey nodded. "Hey, what did you come up here for, Grandpa Hanson? We told Lizzy that we were going for a ride. You didn't think we were lost or anything?"

"No," the old man said, studying the boy. "I came up to talk to you."

Wendy glanced at her grandfather, then at Joey. "I think that's my cue to leave. I'll head on back to the Station. See ya."

Joey waved as his young companion disappeared around the bend. In moments the boy and the old man heard Early's hooves clattering along the road as horse and rider moved through the shadows in the direction of Shadow Creek Ranch.

"Joey," Grandpa Hanson began as the night stillness enveloped them, "it's gone on long enough."

"What has?"

"The trouble between you and Tyler."

Joey leaned against the vehicle and sighed. "Look, Mr. H started it. I didn't."

"He was scared."

The boy gasped. "Scared? Of what?"

"The situation. He'd never had to stop a fight between two people bent on doing bodily harm to each other."

"Well, I didn't start that, either. Tanner did. I was—"

"I know," Grandpa Hanson interrupted. "You were just trying to defend yourself." He rubbed the dent in his hood. "Seems you're doing that a lot nowadays."

Joey grinned. "I really am sorry about that. Guess I was kinda scared. Wasn't thinkin' right." He paused, then he added quietly, "When you're scared, you do stupid things."

Grandpa Hanson nodded. "You get the idea."

The boy walked over to the edge of the road and looked out across the moonlit valley. "Man, I blew it."

"You both did," the old man encouraged. "But the longer you keep out of each other's way, the more it will hurt.

"Ever since Tyler was a little boy he's had a tender

heart. He feels things most of us miss. I could tell he was hurting inside today because of what happened by the footbridge. He loves you, Joey, like you were his own son. I think you know that. But sometimes you gotta make the first move when the other guy is carrying around so much pain in his heart."

Grandpa Hanson glanced up at the stars. "That's what Jesus does for us," he continued. "We're walkin' around all upset over our silly sins, feeling guilty, angry, and He comes to us, with forgiveness in His eyes. He makes the first move, even though He's innocent. He longs to forgive us even before we think to ask."

The old man placed his hand on the teenager's shoulder. "Forgive him, Joey. Don't wait another minute. Please."

Joey nodded slowly. "Mr. H is my friend. He's done a lot of stuff for me. I don't like being mad at him."

"Good. Then talk to him. Sometimes grown-ups can learn a few lessons from kids. Frightening thought."

The boy grinned. "He was scared, huh?"

"Petrified."

Joey took a step forward then paused. "Mr. H is OK. He's really OK."

With a wave, Joey trotted off in the direction of his horse. Grandpa Hanson drove on up the road, looking for a spot to turn around. High above, the Squaw sat silent and still, her eyes dark and brooding, as they had been for centuries.

The morning sun had just risen above the horizon when a gentle knock sounded at Tyler Hanson's bedroom door.

With a moan, the man stirred, then drifted back to sleep.

Again someone knocked.

The lawyer opened one eye and cleared his throat. "Go back to bed, Wendy," he called out. "It's not natural for you to be up so early."

"Hey Mr. H, it's me," a young male voice whispered behind the wooden portal.

Mr. Hanson sat up. "Joey? Is that you?"

"No, it's the boogey man. Can I come in?"

The lawyer grinned. "Sure, come on in."

The door swung open as the teenager entered. He quickly closed it behind him, walked over to the bed, and sat down by Mr. Hanson's feet.

"Good morning, Joey," the lawyer said, unsure of the reason behind the surprise visit. "You sick or something?"

The teenager nodded. "Sorta. I'm sick of us being mad at each other."

Mr. Hanson nodded his head slowly. "Me, too."

"So," Joey continued, "I think we should shake hands and stuff."

"I agree." The lawyer lifted his hand toward the visitor.

With a smile, the boy shook it firmly.

"Joey," Mr. Hanson said softly, "I'm really sorry about what happened. I've been trying to find a moment to talk to you, but one or the other of us is always off doing something. I was going to kidnap you today and drag you off to the pasture for a talk, but you've saved me the trouble."

The teenager chuckled. "Now, that would have looked really good, you dragging me out of the house. Everybody would've figured you were going to finish me off for sure."

Mr. Hanson laughed. "I guess that wasn't such a good idea."

The two sat in silence for a minute. "I understand

about being scared," Joey offered. "Makes you crazy."

"Yeah, it does," the man sighed. "Have patience with me, Mr. Dugan. I'm learning just like you are. But do try to keep that knife of yours out of sight unless you're about to kill a bear or something. Makes me nervous."

Joey nodded. "OK, Mr. H. I guess this is Montana, not New York, right?"

Mr. Hanson rose on one elbow and looked out the window. Bright streams of light spilled down from the distant mountains and poured into the valleys and forests. "No smog, no traffic, no joggers. Yup. Montana."

The boy stood and walked to the door. "I never had nobody get mad at me then feel bad about it." He turned. "Kinda neat."

"Good," Mr. Hanson smiled. "It might happen again, so let me be the first to apologize. Joey Dugan, I'm sorry for the next stupid thing I do."

"Forgiven."

The teenager waved and continued through the door. Closing it behind him, he walked down the hall. His heart felt light, happy. He and Mr. H were friends again. Yes, it felt very good.

CHAPTER FIVE

WORDS OF FIRE

✦✦✦

Ms. Cadena tapped the end of her pencil against the surface of her desk. "Then what did he do?" she asked, pressing the phone closer to her ear. She listened, nodding occasionally. "Oh, my. Oh, dear. Then what did you do?"

Lizzy's voice on the other end of the line continued to recount the goings-on since Ms. Cadena's most recent visit to Shadow Creek Ranch.. After three weeks it seemed everyone was settling in OK, with justs a few mishaps here and there.

Darick and Joey had formed a workable truce between themselves. At least, no knives had been pulled lately. Darick had even taken a shine to mountain climbing.

Joyce and Janet designed and sewed their first sun dresses under Debbie's patient instruction. Ms. Cadena smiled when she heard that Wendy insisted the twins looked like matching candy canes.

Ruben was enjoying anything and everything about the ranch, especially horseback riding. He'd fallen off just once but had jumped right back on. A good sign.

And Andrew insisted on staying close to Mr. Hanson. The boy passed up hikes, games, and trips to the swimming hole. He chose, rather, to work constantly at the lawyer's side. The adults had started calling the lad "Tyler Junior" among themselves.

"Well, I'll be out this afternoon for our next meeting," Ms. Cadena announced with a smile. "Sounds like the kids are having fun."

After a cheery good-bye, Lizzy hung up. Ms. Cadena gently placed her receiver on its cradle and sighed. It was working. Shadow Creek Ranch was working. She rose and walked to the window. Below, Bozeman buzzed with its usual Monday morning activity. Main Street flowed with traffic. Shoppers and businesspeople, along with tourists, hurried from place to place, enjoying the bright Montana sun and warm breezes.

Ruth Cadena rested her head against the cool glass. Her journey had been long, too. She allowed visions from the past to form in her mind: the little village of her birth in the mountains above Mexico City; her father, bone-tired after the day's wheat harvest; her brother, looking proud in his new, freshly-pressed policeman's uniform.

They were gone now—father from a heart attack, proud brother from a drug dealer's bullet. Ruth and her mother had traveled north to Texas, then along the Rocky Mountain backbone of America to Montana, where the young girl had gained citizenship after a long battle with emigration officials.

Mother had returned to the village, to her sisters,

to her past. But Ruth had seen a brighter future among the towering mountains and endless flatlands of Montana.

First, studies at Montana State University on the south edge of Bozeman, then jobs in social service. Two years ago, when she'd heard about Project Youth Revival from a friend, she knew she had found her place in life. The pay wasn't much, but the rewards of seeing young people given a chance to change their perspective was compensation enough.

She smiled to herself. Shadow Creek Ranch was of particular interest to her. Something drew her there, and it wasn't just the beauty of the valley, or the stately Station by the sparkling creek. A strange and wonderful feeling filled her heart each time she steered her little blue station wagon off of Highway 191 and began the slow climb into the Gallatin Mountains.

She laughed softly to herself. No, it was more of a giggle, a little-girl giggle, the kind she used to emit long ago in the mountains of Mexico, when life was safe and warm and the world was filled with loving faces and gentle hands.

* * * * *

"Watch this!" Darick spit on his palms and rubbed them together. Grasping the rope firmly, he backed away from the bank, took a deep breath, and rushed forward.

With a mighty push he propelled himself out over the deep waters. The rope strained under his weight as he swung further and further away from the bank.

A knot, fastened securely above a thick tree limb, creaked and groaned as it tightened its grip. Even the tree seemed to lean back slightly, as if to provide the very best ride for the effort.

Darick swung higher and higher, his legs climbing imaginary steps. He gritted his teeth, fighting the downward force trying to tear his fingers from the thick rope.

Then, suddenly, the force was gone. The boy floated effortlessly in midair for an instant—weightless, unbound by gravity.

Then he began to fall. He pushed the rope away and glanced down between his knees.

Far below, the water waited, as if napping in the afternoon sunshine. Then it began rising to meet him. Faster and faster it came until *splash!* He hit the water hard, bubbles tickling his ears and eyelids.

Even from the depths he could hear the muffled roar of the river as it tumbled over the rocks waiting beyond the deep bowl of the swimming hole. He stopped kicking and let himself drift with the current, suspended in the cool liquid atmosphere.

New York City seemed so far away. The streets, the police sirens, the running feet on midnight sidewalks—they all seemed like a bad dream to him as he floated under the surface of the water.

Everyone on the ranch was being nice to him. It felt good, like he was worth something after all.

The roar grew louder. Maybe he should give a couple of kicks and rise to the surface. But it felt so good down here. The water seemed to be carrying him gently, firmly. He'd wait just a few seconds more.

Darick felt something slam against his chest. Then another jolt forced the small reserve of air from his lungs. The roar was all around him now. He could feel it, not just hear it.

The boy began kicking, but he didn't break through to the surface. He opened his eyes. All he could see was foaming bubbles and dark, shadowy objects moving past at incredible speed.

Realization struck him with a mind-numbing blow. He'd drifted out of the swimming hole into the main current of the river. The roar he heard was the rapids, turning the waters white and angry, throwing it against boulders on its way down the valley toward the falls.

The falls! Darick struggled to find the surface. He must break free. His lungs burned, his chest heaved, instinctively trying to breathe.

For a second, his face was in sunshine. Darick gulped a short breath before the undertow sucked him down again and tossed his twisting, turning body between boulders like it was a rag doll.

The roar was deafening now, and it felt like a whole gang of boys was punching him, jabbing him with sticks, throwing rocks at his arms and legs.

The next instant he was above the water. Beyond the churning surface he caught a glimpse of someone running, stumbling along the river bank. It was Joey. Darick only had time to cry out "HELP!" before the river drew him under again.

Joey's breath came in short, painful heaves as he struggled to keep up with the dark, writhing body out in the river. He knew he must get to his companion before he was swept over the drop.

"Darick!" the runner called, his voice high, strained. "Darick!"

The river ignored the drama being played out below its surface and along its bank. To the waters, it was only natural to rush toward the falls. Gravity dictated it. The fact that a life-and-death situation had developed made no difference. It would continue its journey. It would hurl itself over the lip of the cliff. It would fall unencumbered to the rocks below.

Joey's hands trembled as he ran. He'd told him. He'd told him three times to keep out of the rapids beyond the swimming hole. They'd been here the day before with the whole group. There had been no danger. Now Darick was out in the rapids, being steadily carried toward the falls, toward the unimaginable.

Tears stung the boy's eyes. What would the others say? They'd blame him. They'd say he and Darick had gotten into a fight and somehow, the boy had been captured by the river.

It wasn't true. Sure, they didn't like each other much. Years of street fighting makes people hard, resistant to peace. But they hadn't been fighting. They'd been swinging on the rope at the swimming hole. It was an accident. Just a terrible accident!

The pounding of hooves echoed above the roar of the river. From behind the running boy a horse and rider approached.

"Barry!" Joey screamed as he recognized his friend. "Darick's in the river!"

The wrangler spurred his horse and rushed past the panting boy. In moments he was at the spot where the waters sprayed from the rocks and launched themselves out into empty space.

He quickly dismounted and jumped across the writhing foam, hopping from rock to rock, trying to judge where the boy would be when he arrived at the edge of the bluff.

Joey saw Darick's hand rise weakly out of the waters. Yes! He saw what Barry was trying to do. The wrangler would have one chance to grab the swimmer before he was swept over the falls.

Barry reached up and took hold of an overhanging

limb and leaned out as far as he could toward the rapidly approaching swimmer. Joey skidded to a stop and held his breath. "God. Please. *Please!*"

The wrangler's fingers closed around Darick's upthrust hand. Straining every muscle, the horseman pulled hard as the boy swept past. The swimmer hung for an instant, suspended in air, the torrent plunging past him.

Barry cried out, commanding every ounce of strength he possessed. Darick slammed hard against the rock and dug his free hand into a deep crack in the granite. Slowly, inch by inch, the wrangler dragged the exhausted swimmer up onto the surface of the boulder, and then collapsed beside him.

"Yes! Yes!" Joey jumped up and down, letting out loud war whoops as he ran along the embankment, wildly fanning the air with his arms, a grateful smile creasing his face.

Barry lifted his head and looked over at Darick. The younger boy just nodded and fell back against the stone, too tired to speak.

When strength finally returned to the arms and legs of the pair, Joey helped them stumble to their feet. Cautiously they moved away from the water to higher, safer ground.

There they all tumbled into a heap, happy to know that the river had lost the battle, that Darick would live to face another day.

Joey looked over at his companion. "Hey, Darick," he said softly.

The boy turned.

"Darick, I—"

The teenager lifted his hand. "It wasn't your fault, Joey," he said, as though he could read Joey's thoughts. "You warned me a bunch of times. I just got stupid and forgot."

Joey nodded slowly. "Thanks, Darick," he said. "I'd never want anything bad to happen to you. Never."

Darick smiled. "I know. You're OK, Joey Dugan. You're OK."

Wrangler Barry looked at first one boy then the other. "You two won't be getting married or anything, will you?"

The New Yorkers pummeled the ranch hand with playful fists and shrieks of laughter, their happy mirth blending with the roar of the river as it flung itself over the cliff and dashed onto the rocks far below.

* * * * *

Ruben sat on the pasture fence watching the horses graze by the cottonwoods. He sighed. At that moment he figured he must be the luckiest guy alive. Here he was, under the bright Montana sun, without a care in the world. He didn't have to worry about some gang of frenzied teenagers sneaking up behind him and making trouble. He didn't have to worry about losing his job, because he didn't have one. He didn't have to worry that some policeman would show up and shine a flashlight in his eyes, asking him all sorts of questions about where he'd been and what he'd been doing. The simple truth was, he didn't have to worry. It felt good. Very good.

Ruben lifted the wide-brimmed hat from his head and held it out at arm's length. He loved that hat. Grandpa Hanson had given it to him before the group's first long ride up into the mountains. "Got to keep the sun out of your eyes," the old man had said, "so you can see clearly. Don't want you bumpin' into any trees."

The boy had laughed out loud. He liked doing that.

His grandma had said, even when he was a little baby, he'd laughed a lot. She said he'd just sit in his crib and giggle.

A fly buzzed by. Ruben swatted it away. In his mind's eye he pictured a little kid sitting in a crib, giggling. The thought made him laugh.

"Now that's pretty weird," a voice called from behind.

Ruben turned to see Lizzy approaching, a large bowl of kitchen scraps in her arms.

"What?" the boy asked.

"I'm coming down to the pasture, and I see this guy sitting on a fence laughing. No TV. No radio. No book. He's just sitting there laughing."

A broad smile creased the youngster's face. "So?"

Lizzy lifted the bowl over the fence and let the carrot, apple, and potato scraps cascade to the ground. "So," the woman grinned, "they say that's what crazy people do; sit and laugh at nothing at all. You must be one kooky kid."

Ruben shrugged. "Yup. I am. Never been so crazy in all my life."

Lizzy nodded. "Good. Now I know why you're laughing. I feel better."

The woman turned to leave. "Wait," Ruben called, sliding from his fence-beam perch and falling in step with the old woman. "I want to ask you something."

Lizzy stopped and put down her bowl. "OK," she said as she seated herself beside Shadow Creek. "I've finished my cooking for the day and can now spend some time with crazy people who sit on fences and laugh."

Ruben joined her on the soft grass. "It's kinda serious."

The old woman smiled. "Well, I appreciate you

trusting me with serious stuff. I'll do my best."

The teenager paused, arranging the words he wanted to say as Shadow Creek sang its summer song over the rocks and pebbles at their feet.

"It's about Grandpa Hanson." Ruben picked up a stone and sent it skidding across the water. "When he prays, it's like he's talking to a real person. I've heard other people pray, even preachers, but it's like they're . . . well . . . preaching. But Grandpa Hanson just . . . talks, like we do to each other." The boy scratched his head and looked over at the woman. "Why does he do that?"

Lizzy nodded thoughtfully. "You know, I wondered the very same thing when I came out here last fall. As a matter of fact, I discovered a lot of differences here on the ranch, stuff that was new to me.

"For instance, they don't eat any meat here. I missed it for awhile. But Grandma Hanson taught me how to fix meals that were delicious without a dead animal in sight. She says we should keep ourselves healthy for God. Flesh foods can carry disease. And you know, it works. I do feel better. Maybe it's just country living, but who knows?

"They go to church each Sabbath. I mean, they're really serious about it. Even in the middle of winter, when the snows covered the roads, we'd plow ourselves through somehow.

"And, they do pray a lot; before meals, at bedtime. Yes, Ruben, I've always noticed Grandpa Hanson's prayers. I mean, God listens to us all, but that man's prayers are special. He'll talk to God about anything and everything. It's just like he's speaking to a friend.

"And why shouldn't it be? God says we're suppose to come to Him like we'd come to a friend."

Ruben sighed. "I don't know God all that good," he said.

"That's OK," the old woman encouraged. "He knows you. So you're halfway there."

Lizzy smiled. "Grandpa Hanson says when we pray, we're creating words of fire. He says he likes to think that God takes our prayers and burns them across the sky above His throne in heaven so the whole universe can see that we love Him and want to talk with Him. I like that idea. It makes my little prayers seem more important, more valuable."

"Words of fire," Ruben repeated softly. "Yeah, I like it, too."

"And only a friend would do that for us," Lizzy added. "So, Grandpa Hanson talks to God like He was his friend, which, I guess, He is."

The boy was silent for a minute. "Thanks, Lizzy," he said rising. "I think I understand."

"Good," the old woman responded, stumbling to her feet. "Now you can go back to your fence and laugh some more. I'd better see what Grandma Hanson's up to. If I'd let her, she'd do all the work around here by herself. See ya."

Ruben waved and turned toward the pasture. The horses had gathered around the pile of scraps and were enjoying an afternoon snack. The boy studied the mountaintops and the blue, cloudless sky. "Words of fire," he said thoughtfully.

* * * * *

Joyce glanced up from the sewing machine. "You look pregnant," she giggled.

"I do, don't I?" Janet agreed, twisting from side to side, gazing at her image in the full-length mirror resting in one corner of Debbie's room. "I think I need to take a few more tucks here, here, and here."

Debbie nodded thoughtfully, straight pins protruding from between her teeth. "And you could run a gathering stitch along the seam. With this fabric, that's no big deal."

Janet lifted the dress over her head and smoothed her slip. "Jeans and T-shirts are so much easier to wear."

"Yeah, but bor-ing," Debbie insisted. "Dresses. Now there's fashion."

"You're right," the girl by the mirror sighed.

The trio busied themselves with their projects. Debbie was hemming a cotton-print blouse while Joyce sewed the side seam of a flowing, seersucker skirt. Janet held up her dress and admired its billowy folds. "Sure is pretty," she enthused. "The girls back in New York will think I've been to Paris."

Debbie beamed. It was fun taking nature walks and riding horses. But here, surrounded by the rhythmic cadence of the sewing machine and the flowing lengths of cloth was where she felt most at home. Fashion. She even liked the sound of the word.

"Your dad will think you're beautiful, too," she offered. "My father goes crazy every time I make a new dress. He insists I'm the most beautiful gir—"

Debbie paused, surprised by the frown spreading across her companion's face.

"Janet?" she said softly. "Are you OK?"

The girl turned toward the window. Joyce looked over at Debbie and shook her head, as if in warning.

"Janet, what's the matter?"

The girl by the curtains whirled around. "You keep my father out of this. I don't want to talk about him. You hear me?"

Debbie blinked. "Well . . . sure . . . I . . ."

Janet stood staring across the room, her fists clinched at her side. Joyce sat silent, waiting.

"He's a no good bum. I don't want to look beautiful for him, ever!"

"OK, OK," Debbie pleaded, lifting her hands. "We won't talk about him. I promise."

Tears spilled down the angry girl's cheeks. "As far as I'm concerned, I don't have a father. He's dead. Dead and buried."

Debbie shook her head. "OK. Please, Janet, you're frightening me."

Janet softened a little, then turned back to the window. "I'm sorry, Debbie. You didn't mean any harm. I just don't like to talk about that . . . that monster I'm suppose to call 'Daddy.' No real father would do what he's done."

The girl with the long, dark hair walked over to her companion. "I didn't know," she said softly. "Really."

Janet nodded. "You have no idea how lucky you are," she said without turning. "Your dad loves you. I can tell. I can see it in his eyes. Even when he gets upset with you, there's more hurt than anger in his voice. He thinks you and Wendy are the most beautiful, most wonderful girls in the whole world. That must be neat to have him love you so much."

Debbie nodded. "It is."

"Well, my dad's not like that. No way. When I was a little girl, he started coming into my room and doing stuff, bad stuff. I hated it."

Debbie swallowed hard. "You don't have to tell me this," she said softly.

"I know. But I have to tell someone. I want somebody to feel sorry for me, to cry for me. He never bothered Joyce. She's lucky. It was always me."

Debbie laid her hand on the girl's shoulder. "I can't

imagine what it would be like. I just can't imagine."

Janet gazed into the girl's eyes. "I keep asking myself, 'Am I so impossible to love?' "

Debbie encircled Janet with her arms and wept, her tears mingling with her friend's. They stood together by the window, one trying to understand the unimaginable, the other trying to forget.

When she could speak, Debbie looked into her companion's red and swollen eyes. "Janet," she said, "I love you. We all do. Just know that, OK?"

The girl nodded and smiled through her tears. "Thank you," she said. "It means a lot to me to hear you say that."

Beyond the window, afternoon breezes rocked the leaves of the aspen trees. High above, a hawk soared free, his piercing cry echoing through the valley and across the fields and forests of Shadow Creek Ranch.

"This is suppose to be a ranch." Grandpa Hanson stood on the Station porch, hands on hips. "You know, horseback riding, hikes, camping trips. But Debbie and the twins are cooped up in her bedroom making dresses, Andrew is sitting in front of a computer, Darick and Joey are off swimming in the river, Ruben is perched on top of the fence watching the horses eat, and Wendy and Samantha are at the Bozeman Mall with Tyler. Some ranch."

Grandma Hanson chuckled. "Take it easy, old man," she said. "They're all having a good time."

"Yeah, but whatever happened to that wilderness spirit, that urge to challenge nature with your bare hands?"

The woman shrugged. "I guess kids today need variety. They like to have choices. If they want to challenge nature with their bare hands, I say let 'em, as long as they wash up before supper."

The rancher sighed. "You, too? You're pampering these kids. Why, when I was a lad I—"

"You rode to school on a heated bus and lived in a big house in the city."

The old man nodded. "Oh, yeah. Guess I forgot."

"So quit your belly-aching and finish helping me sweep the porch."

Grandpa Hanson picked up his broom. "Sweep the porch, plug in the toaster, push the buttons on the microwave. Some ranch, I say. Where's the fight for survival, man against beast, eking out a living from the land?"

"Just sweep," the woman commanded. "You can eke later."

With a swish, Grandpa Hanson's broom swept across the wooden slats of the porch and slapped against his wife's posterior.

"Watch it, old man," the woman cried, whirling around. "I've got a broom and I'm not afraid to use it."

The two circled each other, shoulders hunched forward, brooms at ready.

An approaching car interrupted their battle plans. Heralded by the barks of Pueblo the puppy, who by now had grown considerably since he first appeared on the porch, a blue station wagon bumped along the driveway, its driver waving from the front seat. A red minivan followed close behind.

"Well, well," Grandpa Hanson called as he acknowledged the greeting. "My prodigal son returns on the heels of one Ruth Cadena. Do you get the feeling that all these chance meetings aren't just happening by accident?"

"Mind your own business," the woman said without moving her lips. "I thinks she's very nice."

The two walked down the steps and hurried over to

the vehicles. Samantha jumped from the van and held up a package for them to see.

"I got some paints and a dog bone for Pueblo."

Grandpa Hanson scratched his head. "I didn't know that dog could paint."

"No, no," the little girl giggled. "The bone is for my puppy; the paints are for me."

"Oh," the man nodded.

Wendy joined her little companion. "I got a new book, see?"

Grandma Hanson read the title. "*Unexplained Mysteries of the Modern World.* Sounds fascinating."

Mr. Hanson walked over and opened the car door for Ms. Cadena. "Wendy has a one track mind," he sighed. "She keeps asking me about rock formations and ancient images. Like I know about such stuff."

A body appeared on the second floor porch. "Hey, Mr. Hanson," Andrew called, waving a piece of paper above his head. "My mom faxed this afternoon. She bought our idea. It's all set. Now I don't have to be a lawyer. Isn't that neat?"

Grandpa Hanson's eyelids raised. "You talked him out of being a lawyer?"

"I'll explain later," the man said, returning Andrew's wave. "Good work, partner," he called. "Congratulations."

Andrew smiled and disappeared into the office.

The group made their way up the wide stairs and onto the front porch. Evening shadows were beginning to creep across the ranch. It was time for supper, and then there was to be a meeting. Ms. Cadena was anxious to hear reports from the visitors about what they'd been up to.

CHAPTER SIX

RULE NUMBER FOUR

✦✦✦

A deep, mid-morning rumble of thunder shook the Station. Dark clouds skimmed the mountaintops, and a hard rain drummed against the roof. Flashes of lightning illuminated in short, brilliant bursts the miniature rivers that coursed across window panes and the broad porch beams.

The pasture was empty. All the horses had crowded into the corral, trying to escape the downpour.

Shadow Creek surged along its banks, swollen to full capacity by the mountain run-off.

Nine unsmiling, unhappy faces pressed against one of the windows that separated the tempest from the Stations's cozy den. Nine mouths frowned. Nine pairs of eyes watched the sheets of rain wash across the driveway, through the orchard, along the pasture, and into the cottonwoods.

"Well, there goes our ride to Freedom Mountain." Debbie's voice reflected the disappointment all were feeling. "I was looking forward to seeing Red Stone again."

Darick nodded with a sigh. "I like that old man."

"Me, too," added Ruben.

"He tells neat stories," interjected Janet and Joyce.

Joey slumped into his favorite chair by the fireplace. "Rain, rain, rain. Makes Tar Boy look like a drowned rat." He paused. "A really big drowned rat."

Wendy took one last look out the window and dropped into an over-stuffed chair. "And tonight is suppose to be a full moon."

Andrew looked up from his computer magazine. "What's that got to do with anything?"

The girl shrugged and glanced over at Joey. "Oh, we were just going to check on something. No big deal."

Joey's eyelids rose. "Oh, yeah. I forgot." He turned and gazed toward the window. "Now we'll have to wait another month."

"Wait for what?" Debbie pressed, eyeing her friend.

The boy frowned. "I'll tell you later."

Janet and Joyce shuffled across the room and sat down on a big bean bag nestled against one of the tall bookcases. The room fell silent except for the constant drum of the rain.

"Hey, I've got an idea," Debbie called out. "Why don't we play a game?"

No one moved.

"OK, I can see that really got your juices flowing." She thought for a minute. "Then why don't we just talk?"

"About what?" Joey moaned.

"About anything," Debbie pressed, warming to her own idea. "We could discuss politics, or world events, or whatever."

Samantha lifted her hand.

"There," Debbie enthused, "Samantha has a subject she'd like to discuss. She can start us off. What is it you want to talk about, Sam?"

The little girl cleared her throat. "Can I go to the bathroom?"

Laughter erupted across the den as Samantha strode to the door. "I like this game," she called over her shoulder.

Pueblo the puppy jumped up from the spot where he'd been dozing and ran after his mistress. The children heard his happy barks echoing down the hallway.

"Now what do you want to talk about?" Joey queried.

Debbie waved her hand in the air. "Come on, you guys. You know what I mean."

"Hey, I know," Andrew offered, "let's talk about what we're going to do when we're older. Like, I'm going to write software for lawyers—you know, data bases, courtroom reports, stuff like that. Mr. Hanson said there's a big demand for programs lawyers can use. Even my mother thinks it's a good idea."

Wendy leaned forward. "Do you really have to make an appointment to talk to your parents?"

"Yup. It's OK, though." The boy shrugged. "They fit me in whenever they can."

"They fit you in?" Janet cried. "What is this, a business relationship?"

Andrew nodded. "Sort of. They're very busy with real estate planning and investments around Los Angeles. They don't have a lot of time left for me."

"Doesn't that make you mad?" Joyce asked, adjusting her position on the bean bag.

"Well, it used to. Then I talked with some guys at

school whose parents never communicate with them. I mean, it's not like they hate 'em or anything. They just don't have any time. Too stressed out running around making bucks.

"Anyway, those guys feel real hurt and stuff. Kinda angry inside. I just didn't want to feel like that, so I made myself a company of one and I schedule my time with my parents like any other businessman."

"Weird," Wendy said, shaking her head.

"Yeah, it is kinda weird, but it gets the job done."

"So," Joey interjected, "how come they sent you out here? What'd you do, miss an appointment?"

Andrew laughed. "I wish. My friend and I did a very stupid thing. We got some gunpowder from our neighbor, Mr. Harmon—he collects old firearms—and one night we blew a hole in a jewelry store on Rodeo Drive. We were just goofing around. Thought it'd be fun."

The boy scratched his head. "It wasn't a very good idea. My friend got away but I was nabbed at the scene. The police chief said we were lucky we didn't blow ourselves up in the process. Then he told my mom and dad that he was either going to let the press know my identity or they could send me out here for the summer. Guess the old guy figured I'd change my ways if I spent some time on your ranch.

"Well, to make a long story short, here I am, changing my ways in Montana."

Debbie studied the boy thoughtfully. "Are you glad you came?"

Andrew nodded. "Sure. I got to meet Mr. Hanson and all you guys. I'm having a great time."

Darick leaned back in his chair. "I know all about police chiefs," he said with a self-conscious smile. "Captain Abernathy is the one who put me on the airplane. I wasn't too sure I'd like it way out here in the middle of nowhere. Then, as you remember, I got off to a pretty rocky start the very first day I arrived."

Everyone glanced over at Joey. The boy looked around the room. "What?" he commanded.

Darick chuckled. "Mr. Hanson and all the rest have been real nice to me. Even old Dugan over there. I didn't think I'd like it here, you know, all this cowboy stuff. But nobody preaches at me or anything. I got lots of time to think about stuff."

The boy paused. "When I go back, I know the streets will still be there, the gangs, my old buddies. I'll be on my own just like before. But . . ." Darick searched for words. "I'll know there's more. There's more than just the streets. Nobody ever took the time to show me that before."

The group sat in silence for a long moment, listening to the raindrops splashing against the roof. Distant rumbles reminded the occupants of the den that the storm was far from over.

Ruben's hand went up. "I got something to talk about."

Debbie pointed in his direction. "Take it away, Hernandez."

The boy smiled. "I love it here. But I miss my grandmother. She gets sick sometimes. I mean real sick. But I take good care of her. This spring she started coughing and I had to call the ambulance. It was a close one.

"Captain Perry—he's the policeman who told me about the ranch—he said I should just get away from the guys in my neighborhood. But I have no place to go. My grandmother needs me to help her. I don't have any parents. They were killed in a car wreck when I was 3, so I gotta stay right there and tough it out. Some neighborhoods sure make it hard to be good, even if you want to be.

"I don't like getting into trouble. When I can find work, it's a little better. I can buy groceries. But other times, well, you gotta survive, especially when your grandmother's depending on you."

Ruben shook his head. "But I've never seen any place like Shadow Creek Ranch. It's the best. I like the horses and swimming and hiking. Most of all, I like feeling safe, you know, like nobody is going to come up behind you and cause trouble. It's just . . . the best. I'll be sad when I have to go back."

Janet stood, walked to the bookcase, and studied the volumes resting in neat rows. "I'm not going back to my home. No way."

Joyce looked up in surprise. "Well, where we going to live, O Wise One? You got a downtown suite tucked away somewhere?"

The girl fingered a collection of classics. "I'll think of something."

Joyce shrugged. "OK, sis. But I hear the streets get kinda cold around November."

"I don't care," her sister stated flatly.

Joyce leaned her head against the wall. "And food?"

"Look!" Janet whirled around. "We won't starve. We haven't yet. Maybe we can get jobs sewing dresses for rich women or something. Maybe I can stand on a street corner playing the guitar while you sing, *but we're not going back!*"

"OK, OK," Joyce said, lifting her hands in a defensive gesture. "I'm on your side, Janet, remember?"

The girl turned back to the books. "Yeah. We're a team, right?"

"Right."

The gathering fell silent again, each pondering the

woes they faced. After a long moment, Darick spoke. "Man, this rain is making us all feel depressed."

"It ain't the rain," Janet responded with a sigh. "It's life."

Debbie shook her head. "Hey, I didn't mean for us all to get so bummed out."

"Yeah," Joey said, pointing his finger accusingly, "it's your fault. You started all this." A wry smile creased his face. "I think you should be made to stand out in the rain for two days and nights while Pueblo barks at you."

The group laughed as Debbie hid her face in her hands. "Listen," she pleaded, "now that we know what the problems are, let's figure out some solutions. What do you say?"

Heads nodded slowly around the room.

"Good," the girl responded, renewed determination in her voice. "Let's begin with Andrew. First, we should congratulate him on his system of communication. He figured out a way of getting through to his mom and dad, and it works. Good for you."

The group clapped warmly as Andrew stood and bowed. "Thank you, thank you, thank you," he offered. "Leave your gifts at the door."

"But how are we going to keep him from blowing up anymore holes in jewelry stores?"

Andrew lifted his hand. "No problem there. I'm going to be too busy writing software programs. I won't have time to get into trouble."

"All right," Debbie announced, holding up her index finger. "Lesson number one. To keep a teenager out of trouble, make sure he, or she, as the case may be, stays busy doing something else."

"Sounds good," the others chorused.

"Now for Darick's problem," Debbie continued,

"how can we keep him from getting into trouble with his old friends back in New York?"

The kids thought for a minute. Wendy shook her head slowly from side to side. "Sounds like he could use some new friends," she said quietly.

Debbie brightened. She looked around the room, then at her sister. "Out of the mouths of babes," she enthused warmly.

"Hey," Wendy shot back, "who you calling a baby?"

The older girl ignored the retort. "That's a great idea. Darick needs to make new friends, you know, the kind who won't expect you to get into trouble with them."

Darick rolled his eyes. "You mean like those stupid nerds at school who just sit around and talk about science and rockets and junk like that? Get real."

Joey leaned forward. "Hey, Miss Shop-Till-You-Drop may not have such a bad idea. Every school has two basic groups of kids, those who mess around and get in trouble, and those who don't."

"Yeah, they're the nerds," Darick spoke up.

"Some of 'em, but not all of 'em," Joey continued. "And who says you can't start your own gang, but not the kind we've belonged to. This could be a gang who likes certain stuff like, oh, I don't know, sports or music or something."

Darick rubbed his chin. "You mean, like a hobby gang?"

"Yeah," Joey responded. "A group of kids who likes the same things. You could play ball after school, or go places, do stuff. But not bad stuff. You could even set yourself up as a leader and everything."

Darick nodded slowly. "Maybe."

Joey looked around at his listeners. "There even used to be a gang at my old school who rode with younger classmates on the subway to make sure they got home all right. Now there's a good idea. You could sorta be like a safety gang. You'll need some pretty big dudes on your side, but it would work."

Darick grinned. "I know some pretty big dudes. Course, they'd have to be . . . how shall I say . . . persuaded to help out, but I think I can handle it."

Debbie held up a couple of fingers. "Rule number two," she announced. "If your friends are getting you into trouble, make new ones."

Wendy groaned. "Is there going to be a quiz after this is all over?" she asked.

Debbie giggled. "Yes. And an essay paper due in the morning."

"What about me?" Ruben asked excitedly. "How can I help my grandmother best?"

The group leaned back in their chairs. "That's a tough one," Debbie sympathized. "You're doing about all you can do, under the circumstances. I mean, you get jobs, you're trying to stay out of the gangs. I don't know if there's anything more to do."

Ruben's smile faded. "Oh," he said. "I sure wish there was. My grandmother needs me so much. Sometimes I feel like I'm not doing any good at all."

Darick nodded. "But you try, Ruben," he said. "You really try. That's OK in my book."

"Yeah," Joey offered. "It ain't easy in the city. I know. You're doing pretty good, considering."

Ruben brightened. "You really think so? Sometimes I feel kinda lonely, like I'm all by myself in the world. I appreciate what you say. I really do."

Debbie smiled broadly. "Oh, brother," Wendy moaned. "I think rule number three is about to pop up."

"Give me a break," the older sister begged. "I'm just trying to help."

Joey motioned toward the younger sibling. "Don't listen to her, Debbie. What's rule number three?"

"Encouragement," the girl said, holding up her fingers. "We can encourage our friends when they're doing the best they can. We could write them a letter, or call them on the phone. Whatever. But we should encourage, every chance we get."

Darick nodded. "Captain Abernathy keeps telling me how he thinks I can do better, and stuff like that. I thought he was just full of hot air."

"He was following rule number three," Debbie announced triumphantly.

Heads nodded around the room.

Janet ran her fingers through her hair and sat up. "OK, Debbie Hanson," she said. "How 'bout me and Joyce? What rule can you make that will help in our situation? You know what's waiting for us back in New York. What are you supposed to do when your worst nightmare lives in the same house with you?"

Debbie looked down at her feet. "I . . . I don't know," she said softly. "Oh, Janet, I've thought about it a lot. Sometimes I lie awake at night and worry about you and Joyce and . . . your situation. But I don't have any rules for what you face. It just makes me cry."

Janet stood and walked across the room. "Yeah, well, we can take care of ourselves. Don't lose any sleep over us. We'll survive, even if it kills us."

The girl turned and strode through the door, leaving the room silent. Debbie studied the patterns on the rug. Was there no rule, no help, no way out for Janet and her sister?

She glanced over at Joey. He shook his head slowly. It seemed some things were beyond understanding, even for those who were trying to help.

In the weeks that followed, the inhabitants of Shadow Creek Ranch found ample time to explore every mountain fold and grassy valley within riding distance of the Station.

Each day brought new discoveries in the world of nature, breath-taking vistas, and abundant opportunities to build mind and body.

Wendy was pleased at the way her students had learned to control the beautiful animals they rode each afternoon. Her young heart filled with pride when she witnessed the careful, loving attention paid to the ranch horses.

Wrangler Barry kept a close eye on the goings on, making sure safety rules were kept to the letter.

Mealtime remained a favorite among the guests and residents alike. Happy banter, good-natured kidding, and a constant stream of laughter made the food Lizzy and Grandma Hanson prepared taste even better.

But, as the days flew by, Janet became more and more withdrawn. She would be found sitting alone by the creek in the evening shadows, or out on long early-morning walks up the valley road.

Debbie noticed it first. It worried her tender heart.

"Father?" Her soft voice called from the doorway leading into Mr. Hanson's office one morning. "Can I talk to you, alone?"

Andrew looked up from his keyboard. "Something tells me I'd better save my work and go play catch with Wendy and Ruben."

Mr. Hanson smiled. "Thanks, partner. When my eldest daughter calls me 'Father' I know something important is on her mind. I'll let you know if any faxes come in from your parents."

The youngster waved and exited the room, smiling over at Debbie as he went by.

"Nice kid," the lawyer said with a satisfied grin. "I like him. He's going to do great things in the future."

Debbie nodded. "He sure knows his computers."

Mr. Hanson pointed toward an empty office chair. "Park it there, girl, and tell me what's on your mind."

Debbie sat down and glanced out the window. "See that?" she asked.

"What?"

"Over there, at the far end of the pasture, by the cottonwoods."

The lawyer gazed out beyond Shadow Creek, across the green pasture, to where a stand of trees guarded the east end of the expanse. He could see a figure walking slowly among the slender trunks.

"That Janet or Joyce?"

"Janet," Debbie said softly.

"How can you tell?"

"I don't know. I just can." The girl looked into her father's eyes. "Daddy, I want to help her but I don't know how. I'm sure she's worried about going back to New York. I see fear in her eyes. Real, deep fear."

The lawyer sighed. "I know. Ms. Cadena has told us about her situation at home. It makes me sad, too."

"But can't anything be done?"

Mr. Hanson ran his fingers through his hair. "Ruth said she talked to Janet a few weeks ago, but the girl doesn't trust her. I mean, she likes Ms. Cadena and all, but she feels all adults are out to get her or something. Can't say I blame her. All the adults in her life have either abandoned her or . . ." The man hesitated. "Or worse."

Debbie shook her head. "Well, who does she trust?"

Mr. Hanson smiled. "As I see it, other than her

sister, she has only one true friend in the world."

"Who?"

"A beautiful young girl living on a ranch in Montana."

The teenager gasped. "Me?"

"Yup. You've been a real friend to Janet. She admires you. You've taken time to get to know her and Joyce. I think she trusts you. You're going to have to be the one to help her."

"But I don't know how," the girl groaned. "If I knew, I would."

Mr. Hanson pointed toward the phone. "Why don't you call Ms. Cadena? She's expecting to hear from you."

Debbie blinked. "She is?"

The man turned and walked back to his desk. "Ruth is a very perceptive woman. She knows not to step in where she's not welcome. For weeks now, she's realized the deep friendship you and Janet have formed and has been waiting for you to come to the point where you want to help. She's got some ideas to share. Call her. It'll make her day."

Debbie's lips lifted in a tiny grin. "Perceptive, huh? Pretty, too, wouldn't you say?"

Mr. Hanson blushed slightly. "Now, Deborah Sue. What are you inferring?"

"Oh, nothing," the girl chuckled. "I have my perceptions, too. And I know my handsome father gets a little lonely from time to time."

The lawyer picked up the phone and handed it to his daughter. "Just call the woman," he said. "The number's there on the desk."

"How convenient," the teenager giggled.

Mr. Hanson rolled his eyes and returned to his work. He typed a few words on the keyboard, then glanced back at Debbie. They both burst out laughing.

"You're impossible!" he moaned. "Just dial the stupid phone, OK?"

Debbie's fingers pressed the buttons, a broad smile creasing her face. In moments she heard a cheery hello. Glancing out the window, toward the pasture, she began speaking slowly into the receiver.

* * * * *

The afternoon sun felt warm on Janet's face. Midday meal chores were finished. Wendy and the others were saddling up their horses for a ride down to the river, and the adults had all returned to their tasks in and about the Station.

The girl's forehead wrinkled slightly. What was Debbie up to? She'd been very mysterious all during lunch. Said she wanted to take her somewhere secret, a place no one knew about except her and Grandpa Hanson.

Janet grinned. That Debbie. Always something up her sleeve.

"Ready to go?" Janet looked up to see her friend approaching, two saddled horses in tow.

"Sure thing," the girl smiled. "Where we off to?"

Debbie leaned forward and whispered. "It's a secret."

"Right," Janet responded with a wink.

In minutes they were moving along a forest path. Bright sunshine filtered through the pines, forming yellow pools of light on the soft soil below their horses' hooves.

On and on they went, higher and higher up the mountain, each enjoying the quiet solitude of the deep forest. After 30 minutes or so Debbie reined in her horse. Janet rode up beside her.

"We there?" the girl asked, looking around.

"Just about," Debbie said. "First, I want to tell you something. My grandfather brought me up here last spring. It's a very special place only we know about. Now, I'm going to show it to you because you're my friend."

Janet smiled shyly. "Hey, thanks, Debbie. I know I'll like it."

"Good. Just head down the path another 50 feet and we'll be there. You go first."

The two riders continued along the trail. Pushing aside a low-lying branch with her arm, Janet suddenly found herself on the shore of a sparkling mountain lake.

Her breath caught in her throat as Debbie rode past and guided her horse along the water's edge toward a clearing to the right.

"See what I mean?" she called over her shoulder. "Neat, huh?"

"It's beautiful!" Janet gasped as she surveyed the delicate, tree-lined curves of the distant shore and the clear, spring-fed waters sweeping out in front of her. "It's just beautiful!"

"He calls it Papoose Lake," Debbie said, slipping from the saddle and tying up her steed by a fallen log. "Grandpa says it's his favorite place in the whole world. Mine, too."

Janet guided her mount over to join her companion. "And no one knows about it? Just you and Grandpa Hanson?"

"And now you," Debbie enthused. "Just us three. That's why it's a secret."

The two girls sat down on the log and gazed out over the waters. A chorus of insects sang their summer song into the warm breezes that skipped across the lake, leaving tiny ripples in their wake.

Debbie looked at her companion. "I wanted to discuss something with you," she said quietly. "Something important."

Janet nodded. "OK. Shoot."

Debbie reached into her pocket and pulled out a piece of crumpled paper. She handed it to her friend.

"What's this?" Janet asked, studying a name and some numbers scrawled across the parchment.

"It's the telephone number of a family in New York."

"So?"

Debbie paused. When she spoke, her words were carefully chosen. "They want you and Joyce to come live with them. They have a big house and no children of their own. He's a retired electrician and she teaches piano lessons in the afternoons."

Janet studied the paper in her hand. "Cadena?" she asked.

"Well, she gave me a list of names and I called them all. This is the one that sounded the best to me."

The girl looked up. "You called a bunch of people in New York?"

"Yes." Debbie licked her lips nervously. "I spent the morning in my dad's office. Janet, please, call them. Talk to them. They work closely with Project Youth Revival. They've had kids come and live with them before. They understand what you're going through at home, with your father and all.

"I'm sorry if I'm butting in where I don't belong, but I care about you and Joyce. I want you to be happy, safe. Forgive me if I'm out of line, but I can't help it. You're my friend. I don't want any more bad things to happen to you. You can't do it alone. You need someone. I want to be that someone, if you'll let me."

A tear slipped from Janet's eyes and slid down her cheek. "You did this for me? You called people all morning?" she asked softly.

"My dad's going to love his phone bill," Debbie grinned. "Some of those people would talk your leg off if you let them."

Janet looked over at her friend. A shadow of fear moved across the young girl's face. "What if they—"

"He won't," Debbie answered her unfinished question. "Not all men are like your dad. Most are kind and loving. You've got to believe that, Janet. You have to believe that there are good people out there, people who are willing to care about you in a pure and wonderful way."

Debbie saw her companion tremble just a little. "I'm scared," Janet said.

Placing her arm around the girl's sagging shoulders, Debbie looked into her eyes. "You can't stay at home anymore. You just can't."

In the distance a rainbow trout leaped into the air and snagged a bug on the wing. With a quiet splash it fell back below the glassy surface of the lake, sending a circle of ever-widening ripples across the waters.

"I'll send you a letter every week," Debbie encouraged. "When the weather's not too cold, I'll come up here and write. This will be our log, our shore." She paused. "I'll never forget you Janet. I'm your friend for life."

Janet lifted the wrinkled scrap of paper and studied it for a long moment. Then she folded it neatly and slipped it into her shirt pocket.

"OK," she whispered. "If you think it's what I should do."

Debbie squeezed the girl's hands tightly. "It is."

Janet chuckled softly to herself. "What's so funny?" Debbie asked.

The girl looked out across Papoose Lake. "We found it."

"What?"

Janet turned and faced her friend. "Rule number four."

"Rule num—?" Realization crept into the teenager's mind. "Oh yes, our rainy day talk."

Janet rose. "Rule one, keep out of trouble by keeping busy. Rule two, find friends who won't make you do things you don't want to do. Rule three, always encourage other kids who are having a rough time." Janet picked up a rock and sent it skipping over the water. "And rule number four, let other people help you. Don't go it alone. Right?"

Debbie stood also, and surveyed the distant trees. "That's the very lesson I learned the first time Grandpa brought me up here," she said softly. "Must be something in the air."

The two mounted their horses and rode to the edge of the forest. They disappeared among the trees, leaving Papoose Lake peaceful and still under the afternoon sun.

CHAPTER SEVEN

SHADOWS ON THE CLIFFS

✦✦✦

The airport terminal swarmed with activity as tourists and business travelers purchased tickets and checked their baggage at the airline counters.

The group from Shadow Creek Ranch huddled together at one corner of the glass-lined waiting room, exchanging hugs and handshakes.

Andrew had convinced his parents not to send the company jet to Bozeman. It would be waiting for him in Salt Lake City, where his companions would be meeting their connecting flights.

"Thanks, Mr. Hanson," the young teenager offered, hand outstretched. "I really liked your ranch."

The man bypassed the handshake and gave the boy a big hug. "I'm going to miss you, partner," he said. "My computer equipment won't work right without you around." Mr. Hanson smiled. "I'll be looking for your very first software program. Don't make it too hard for fumble-fingered lawyers like me to understand."

"Don't worry," Andrew beamed. "I'll make the interface nice and easy."

Ruben saddled up to Wendy. "Hey, I enjoyed your riding lessons," he said, a shy grin lighting his face. "Take good care of those animals for me."

Wendy nodded. "Sure thing, Ruben. I'll give your horse an extra apple everyday and tell him it's from you."

Nearby, Darick stood with Joey watching the jets and commuter planes move across the airport ramp. "Someday I'm going to fly airplanes," the dark-skinned boy announced.

"You are?"

"Yup. I like riding in them. So much power out there on the wings." He paused. "You know, Dugan, I never thought we'd be friends because of what happened in the city and all, but I was wrong. People can change if they want to. You did."

Joey nodded. "It ain't easy. But it's possible. I'm glad we decided not to kill each other." He lifted his hand. "Good luck on the streets, man."

Darick gripped Joey's fingers. "Thanks. I'll need it."

Debbie, Ms. Cadena, and the twins stood in a tight circle, talking among themselves.

"And guess what they did last week," Janet was saying.

"What?" Debbie asked expectantly.

Janet leaned forward. "Mrs. Tomlinson went out and bought a sewing machine. Just like yours. Isn't that neat? See, they sent me the owner's manual. I can continue making dresses right in our new home. They said in their letter that they're going to meet me and

Joyce at the airport this afternoon. I'm a little nervous, but Mrs. Tomlinson said she was too, so we'll be nervous together. Isn't this just about the neatest thing you ever heard?"

Debbie nodded, a tear shining in one corner of her eye. "Oh, Janet," she said, "you're going to love it in your new home. I just know you will. You can design dresses and send me pictures and everything. It's so wonderful!"

The two girls jumped up and down and hugged each other tightly. Glancing over at Ms. Cadena, Janet smiled. Her lips moved, wordlessly forming the words, "Thank you."

The woman winked and added her arms to the happy hug.

Suddenly, the loudspeaker above their heads crackled to life. "Your attention, please. Flight 1201 to Salt Lake City with connections to Denver, Chicago, and New York is now ready for boarding at gate two. All passengers holding confirmed seats should be in the boarding area at this time."

Tears and smiles spread through the group as promises to write and remember were exchanged. Then Shadow Creek Ranch's very first summer guests were gone, into the sky on silver wings.

Debbie waved until the airplane was just a speck in the southern sky. Then she turned and ran to her father. Throwing her arms around him, she cried tears of joy.

When she could speak, she looked up into the man's eyes. "Daddy, I love you," she said. "Thank you for loving me."

Mr. Hanson nodded. He understood the full meaning of his child's words. With a grateful smile he pressed the girl close to his heart as father and daughter rejoiced that theirs' was a special relationship, the kind the Creator had in mind when He first made man, and then blessed him with the beautiful gift of a baby girl.

* * * * *

It was time. A full moon hung above the mountains like a distant beacon, leading the truck along the bumpy road.

The story of the Squaw had been murmured in the hallways and muttered under napkins during dinner conversations long enough. It was time to leave the safety of the valley, to stand under the towering formation, to witness the mysterious lights, and to listen for the whispers in the wind.

Grandpa Hanson guided the vehicle along the old logging road, doing his best to keep one eye on the trail and the other up above, where even now the formation was coming into view.

"Look," Joey said. "There are shadows on the cliffs. See 'em?"

Wendy nodded. "Yeah. Just like before."

Debbie rolled down her window and cupped her hand over her ear. "No whispers yet," she reported.

Joey rolled his eyes. "I know you don't believe us, so just don't make fun, OK?"

"OK," the girl agreed, trying to suppress a giggle.

"Besides," the boy continued, "you're the one who begged to come with us tonight. You could've stayed home with the other doubting Thomases. Your dad and Grandma Hanson think we're all nuts anyway. Even Lizzy wasn't any too excited about our adventure. So lighten up!"

"Isn't that what the rock is suppose to do?" the girl queried, forcefully keeping back more giggles.

Grandpa Hanson lifted his hand. "Come on, you

guys. Quit pestering each other. We're almost there."

The truck ground to a halt at the spot Wendy and Joey determined was the exact same place they had seen the mysterious light in the image's eyes two months before.

Silently everyone piled out of the vehicle and stood by the road, gazing intently at the formation.

Joey checked his watch, holding it up to the light of the moon. "Yup. This is it. This is precisely the time we were here."

The group stood in the middle of the road, staring up at the Squaw.

"I don't see anything but a rock formation," Debbie yawned. "You guys were just imagining things that night. Come on. I'm getting chilly. Let's go ba—"

The word stuck in the girl's throat as the Squaw's eyes began to glow.

"There! See? Do you see it?" Joey screamed. "Tell me you see it!"

Grandpa Hanson's mouth dropped open. "Well I'll be a jackrabbit's hind leg. They are shining. Look at that."

Debbie backed away slowly. "Hey. What's going on? How'd you do that?"

"We didn't do anything," Joey said, his eyes fixed on the Squaw's. "I told you. I told you! Now do you believe me?"

Grandpa Hanson stepped forward. "Let's go find out what it is."

"No way," Wendy responded, her voice shaking. "I'm not going up there."

Grandpa Hanson kept on going. "Come on. There's nothing to be scared of. I'm sure we'll find a logical explanation for . . ."

The man stopped. "Oh, they went out."

Wendy blinked. "No, they didn't. See? They're still shining."

Grandpa Hanson looked up at the dark eyes of the squaw. "But they're not shining where I'm standing." He moved back down the path toward the others. Slowly the eyes began to glow again, their evil gaze studying him thoughtfully.

The old man paused and rubbed his chin. Then a tiny smile began to play at the corners of his mouth.

"Come on, you guys," he called, starting up the trail once more. "I think I have the answer."

Joey edged forward. "OK, I may as well die here as somewhere else," he announced. He lowered his head and starting running after Grandpa Hanson. Glancing up again, he noticed that the eyes had stopped glowing. Pausing, he backed up. Sure enough, just as the old man had discovered, the light returned.

By now, Grandpa Hanson was clamoring up the side of the formation, grabbing hold of rocks and shrubs, inching his way along the arm of the Squaw.

"Hey, wait for me!" Joey called.

Together the two explorers eased themselves up to the formation's shoulders, then carefully moved to the broad outcropping forming the head. Taking hold of a sturdy branch, Grandpa Hanson leaned around and looked straight into the rough and weather worn face of the image.

He stayed there, suspended in space, above the squaw's chest and lap.

When he swung back to the shoulder, he was carrying something in his hand. "Take a look at this," he told Joey, handing him a heavy object.

The boy held a large rock up into the moonlight. Its shiny, red surface sparkled, reflecting the lunar glow like a mirror.

"Now, swing out there and see for yourself," Grandpa Hanson urged.

Joey obeyed. What he saw made him almost lose his grip and tumble headlong toward the valley floor. There, in the area forming the big eyes of the Squaw, was a vein of glowing rocks, like the one he clutched in his free hand. The cavity was filled with this kind of stone, their surfaces forming a thousand shining mirrors, each one catching the rays of the full moon and intensifying the glow.

Joey gasped. A reflection. It was only a reflection of the full moon on the rocks.

The boy began to chuckle. Then he burst out laughing, his voice echoing across the valley floor.

Debbie and Wendy looked at each other, then up at the glowing eyes. They could see a figure moving inside the light.

"Joey!" Wendy called. "Are you all right? What do you see?"

"Rocks," came the happy reply. "Shiny rocks. Lots of them. It's like a mirror up here."

Grandpa Hanson and the boy clamored down the formation and hurried to join their companions.

They stood together looking up at the eyes. Then slowly, as the moon continued its journey through the night sky, the light faded until the Squaw sat once again in darkness.

Joey spun around and pointed his finger skyward. "*The moon!* It's just a reflection of the moon!"

"And when the moon is full," the old man continued, "it shines the brightest. And right here on this spot is where the reflection is concentrated the most this time of year."

Wendy frowned. "You mean there're no ghosts or anything?"

Grandpa Hanson leaned against the truck. "Funny how the human mind has been conditioned. The old devil makes sure we hear just enough stories of unexplained phenomena, just enough tappings and rappings and sounds in the dark, that we begin to believe a rumor he started 5,000 years ago.

"He said people don't really die. He insisted that they lived again in some wonderful far-off world, or walked around ours, haunting the living. It's just not true. It's a lie, plain and simple."

Wendy lowered her head. "So the dead are really dead? Rats."

"You know they are, Wendy Hanson," the old man said. Then he leaned forward. "But there's going to be a time when dead people will rise from their tombs and walk around."

Joey's eyes opened wide. "When?"

"At the second coming of Jesus. Says so in the Bible. But these ghosts won't be evil apparitions saying 'boo' to everyone. They'll be perfect human beings, free from sin and suffering, free to roam the universe with the angels. That's the only ghost story you ever need to hear."

Grandpa Hanson and the children took their places in the ranch truck. Slowly the old man turned the vehicle around and bumped back down the road toward the valley and the Station.

The secret of the Squaw had been unmasked. And like so many secrets, the answer had not only illuminated the truth for today, but had also shone into the future, to a brighter tomorrow.

That's when all people, young and old, will be free from fear. They will soar like the angels, filling their minds with wonderful truths as they travel across the limitless space of God's glorious universe.